A Foul and Fearsome Tail

A Sassy Sarcastic Cat Cozy Mystery

Rachel Woods

BONZAI
MOON

BonzaiMoon Books LLC
Houston, Texas
www.bonzaimoonbooks.com

Hey, y'all, hey!!!

Subscribe to my newsletter and you'll get inspiring rescue stories, hilarious cat memes, and thrilling serialized fiction. Plus, you can find out first about new books featuring my fabulous life as a feisty, fierce feline, and much more!

Sign me up!

Sassy Callie

https://subscribepage.io/SassyCallie

Prologue

Since the unfortunate incident, which occurred roughly two months ago, during which I was unceremoniously and without provocation attacked by Callie, the Calico cat who suffers from selective catnesia —which, according to the cat is a feline form of amnesia—my life continues to evolve.

How, you may be asking? Or, maybe you're not asking. Perhaps you're merely wondering. Or pondering. Or hoping I just get on with telling you how my life has evolved.

Yes. Right. Well. So …

Firstly, I am continuing my quest to become the world's greatest investigative reporter. An ambitious feat, I know, but I am absolutely up for the challenge.

Of course, my boss, Martin "Marty" Edwards, the editor of the newspaper where I work as a Junior Reporter, is not exactly impressed with my reporting. He's on a grand quest to fire me for various reasons, including but not limited to the fact that my writing is not always exciting or inspiring, and sometimes, I leave out certain details that are critical to my stories. Unfortunately, I can't dispute that criticism. But I assure you, I am doing much better at making sure I get all the detailed details.

Marty doesn't think I have what it takes to be a great reporter. That is, he doesn't think I have "it." According to Marty, "it" is comprised of the following: skills, talent, fortitude, and basic common sense. Marty doesn't think I have any of "it" and he says I don't even know how to get "it."

I beg to differ.

Maybe I don't have all of "it."

But, I have some of "it."

Now, which of "it" I have, I am not quite sure but if I had to guess —and I do love a good guessing game—I would guess that I have basic common sense or fortitude. Perhaps both.

Admittedly, my skills and talent are lacking at the moment. But that's okay because I might not write the best articles or speculate to the correct conclusion, but I have something to help me overcome my deficiencies.

What is this something, you may be wondering?

Well, it is none other than a talking cat.

Yes, a talking cat. I have a talking cat. Well, correction, I *know* a talking cat. Her name is Callie. She's the Calico I mentioned earlier, the one who attacked me. For no reason. And put me in a coma. Again, for no reason. Although to be fair, Callie didn't put me in a coma. An allergic reaction to antibiotics did that, however, I suppose if Callie hadn't attacked me, I wouldn't have needed antibiotics, so …

Anyhoo, Callie is not my cat, but I am her human. I know, I know. It's complicated, but it's for the best. Suffice it to say, Callie is one of the reasons my life has evolved.

Because of the cat's help, I have been able to solve not one, but two, murder mysteries. After solving the murders, I wrote articles about my investigations, and while the writing left much to be desired, the first-hand accounts of my adventures were riveting and enthralling. My stories trended online and helped me keep my job, much to Marty's chagrin.

So, it should not surprise you that my life, and possibly my career, might sort of suck if the cat was no longer around.

Unfortunately, the one thing I'm dreading could happen.

I might have to give up Callie.

That is, I might have to return her to her real human. The person she belongs to. Her rightful owner. Because of the selective catnesia, Callie has no idea who her real pawrents are. She asked me to help her find out more about her past, which I did. After a visit to the vet, I discovered Callie had been microchipped. The vet gave me the name of Callie's owner.

"I know who your real owner is … "

"Who is it, sis?"

I give her the name.

"Doesn't sound familiar," said the cat.

"Well, would it? Considering your catnesia."

"Suppose you're right," said the Calico.

"Now I guess we just need to contact your real owner."

"Yeah. I guess so, sis …"

But we haven't done that yet.

I got super busy writing stories and Callie has been off doing what she does best—being independent.

Now, the time has come for me to return her to her rightful owner.

There's only one problem. Wait, two problems. No, there's just one problem. I don't know if I want to return Callie to her real owner. Oh, what am I thinking? I absolutely do not want to return Callie to her owner. In the short time I've known her, and despite the fact that she attacked me and sent me to the hospital, I've become super attached to her. I don't think I can give her away and never see her again.

But, I don't have a choice.

I promised Callie I would reunite her with her real owner.

Even though it will break my heart, that's what I'm going to do.

Chapter 1

At eight o'clock on a humid, blustery morning threatening rain—which is disappointing for the thousands of tourists who woke up this morning hoping for sunshine and blue skies, which is what the Palmchat Islands, were I was born, raised, and currently reside, are celebrated, and adored for—I am not doing what I wish I could be doing.

I'd love to be sitting at my desk in my cubicle checking my social media feeds while fact-checking my latest articles. This potentially arduous task would be completed with the help of mint and pineapple tea and mango and guava glazed donut holes, one of my favorite and most cherished tea-and-donut holes combinations.

Instead, I am sitting in my boss's office, slumped in the chair on the opposite side of his desk, trying not to cringe as he delivers a stinging, withering rebuke of my latest investigative reporting efforts.

Marty is a short, squat man, built like a body-building gymnast with stiff blonde hair sprouting from his bald scalp like straw. His pale complexion, not suited for a tropical island climate, is usually flushed and pink. At times, his sweaty face reddens, making him resemble a tomato, a fire hydrant, a lobster, a drop of dried blood, a strawberry, a chili pepper, or various and sundry other red items. These times normally happen when he's irritated or frustrated with me.

"Sophia..." begins Marty, his world-weary tone laced with annoyance. "First of all, let's start with something positive, even though that will be a stretch."

"Something positive is always a good way to start," I agree, smiling, determined to display a sunny disposition, which will match the yellow blazer I've chosen to wear over a sleeveless pink sheath dress.

"According to the latest weather forecast," says Marty, "the rain should only last about an hour or so and then we'll have sunny skies for the rest of the day."

"That's good," I say, happy that the day won't be a total rain-out and vacationers will have the chance to enjoy a lovely day in St. Mateo.

"Now that we've had our moment of positivity," says Marty. "Let's move on to the negative news."

"Negative news about what?"

"About you."

Confused, I ask, "Negative news about me? I don't understand. How are we already at the negative news? What was the positive news?"

"It's not going to rain all day."

"And that's great," I agree. "But, I meant, what's the positive news about me?"

"Sophia ..." Marty gives me a grim smile. "Why would you think there would be any positive news about you?"

"Because you said you were going to start with the positive."

"Yes, I did say that," says Marty. "But I didn't say the positive news would be about you."

Crestfallen, I nod. "Oh. Okay. Well, um. I just thought—"

"And that's the main problem with you," says Marty. "You think. And that's not a good thing because your thoughts are chaotic, sporadic, and nonsensical."

"Chaotic, sporadic, and nonsensical," I repeat, trying not to feel glum and defeated.

"And that's me being generous."

Again, I'm flummoxed. "Generous how?"

Marty exhales. "Sophia, I suppose you think because you were instrumental in solving two murders that I'm going to overlook or excuse your bad reporting but I am even less inclined to give you kudos, particularly following your recent articles."

"And which recent articles are you referring to?" I ask.

"Let's start with the woman who called the police to report that her roommates were plotting to kill her."

Nodding, I say, "Wasn't that terrifying? I mean, you think you know people, right?"

"What's terrifying is that you forgot to mention in your article that the roommates were not people."

"Right," I say, recalling the sinister story.

Marty scowls at me. "The woman—a lonely widow—referred to her house plants as her roommates."

"Right," I say, nodding.

"But you didn't tell me that when you pitched the story to me," says Marty, his skin starting to redden and possibly blister. "You made me think that this poor, old widow was being targeted."

"She was being targeted," I insist.

"But not by people!" thunders Marty.

"Okay, well, yes, that's true," I acknowledge. "However, just because she wasn't being threatened by people doesn't make her experience any less harrowing."

"Are you being serious right now?" demands Marty. "Are you, with the majority of your faculties intact, claiming that people should be afraid of hibiscus and bird of paradise?"

"Actually, it was hibiscus and oleander," I correct him. "Birds of paradise are docile plants and never seek to maliciously or with forethought do any harm. However, oleanders are violently poisonous and hibiscus can be manipulated into carrying out barbaric acts."

Pinching the bridge of his nose, Marty shakes his head.

"People should know that plants can be beautiful and deadly," I continue. "Just because plants don't announce their evil intentions does not mean that they aren't secretly strategizing our downfall."

"And why would a house plant want to secretly strategize our downfall?"

"Well, probably because the house plant doesn't want to be a house plant," I say. "I mean, think about it…"

"I'd rather not," mumbles Marty, dropping down into his chair, causing the leather to creak and whine in protest.

"Would you like to spend the rest of your life confined to a pot, generally no larger than seven inches in diameter, doomed to live indoors, never experiencing the warmth of the sun on your leaves?"

Scratching his head, Marty says, "Why did I even ask?"

"Didn't you want to know?"

"Let's discuss this story about the local cricket team being hypnotized to lose games," says Marty.

Shuddering, I say, "Isn't that so shady and scary and sinister?"

"But is it true?"

"The hypnotist admitted to hypnotizing the team members," I say. "When the team members hear the phrase, ala peanut butter sandwiches … or, is it supercalifragilisticexpialidocious?"

"So, it's either Sesame Street or Mary Poppins?"

"One of the two," I say. "Anyway, when the team members hear the phrase, they should go into a catatonic trance, which will stop them from playing the game, and thus the opposing team will win."

"But the local cricket team has a winning record."

"I know!" I say, smiling and clapping my hands. "Isn't it exciting! They are undefeated!"

"Then how are they being hypnotized to lose?"

"Well, obviously, the hypnosis is not working," I say.

"Exactly," says Marty. "But you didn't bother to point that out in your article."

Confused, I ask, "I didn't? Are you sure?"

"If you had, the local cricket team would not be threatening to sue us!"

"Sue us?" I gasp. "Why?"

"Are you seriously asking me—with what little remains of your feeble mind—why the cricket team is threatening to sue us?" demands Marty, his face practically glowing red, like a glaring traffic light. "You seriously don't understand why your story was libelous?"

Biting my lip, I say, "Well, um, I suppose …"

"Never mind." Marty slouches back in his chair. "I want you to write a retraction."

"A retraction?"

Marty's shrewd eyes narrow. "You know what that is?"

"Well, um, I suppose …"

"Forget it," barks Marty through gritted teeth. "I'll write the retraction myself. And this is what you are going to do …"

Excited, I ask, "What's that?"

"First of all," begins Marty, "I want you to know that I regret that I have to continue to allow you to work at this paper, particularly when I don't believe you deserve this job, however, Vivian likes you."

"And I like her, as well," I say, thinking about my mentor, Vivian Thomas-Bronson, the beautiful former ex-war correspondent. She's an award-winning journalist who enthralled the world with her poignant writing and cunning investigative skills.

Vivian manages the *Palmchat Gazette* from its main office in St.

Killian, which is where I used to live before I took the job Vivian offered me at the *Palmchat Gazette* satellite office in St. Mateo.

"For some reason—mind-altering drugs come to mind—Vivian thinks that with time, patience, and good coaching, you'll become a great reporter," says Marty.

Recognizing the skepticism in his gaze, I say, "And, of course, you don't think I have a goat of a chance."

Marty frowns. "You mean … a ghost of a chance."

Frowning back at him, I shake my head. "No, I meant … a goat of a chance."

"And what does that mean?"

"It means the goat doesn't have a chance."

"A chance at what?"

"At winning," I say.

Marty's face turns tomato red. "Winning what?"

"The race."

"What race?" demands Marty, his face as flushed and crimson as a cooked lobster.

"The goat race," I say.

Marty scowls. "Are you doing this on purpose, Sophia?"

"Doing what on purpose?"

"Being completely and irrevocably nonsensical!"

"What's nonsensical about a goat race?"

Rubbing his eyes, Marty exhales slowly. "Never mind. Doesn't matter. Okay. I'm sending you out on a story."

"What's it about?" I ask, anxious for a new assignment and another chance to prove to Marty, once and for all, that I am a good reporter and I do have "it."

"A young woman was found dead this morning at Copper Beach Dog Park."

"How terrible," I exclaim.

"I want you to get over to the dog park, get the details, get a statement from the cops, get comments from any witnesses, and then I want a first draft on my desk by the end of the day. Understood?"

Smiling, I say, "Absolutely!"

"And it goes without saying yet it does bear repeating," says Marty. "Do not blow it, Sophia. I will ship you out if you don't shape up!"

Chapter 2

The Copper Beach Dog Park is a place I know fairly well, even though I don't have a dog.

A good friend of mine, Noah Cuetee, who happens to be a police officer with the St. Mateo police department, and my secret confidential source, has a canine partner. Officer Cuetee's dog is a Belgian Malinois named Dutiful who is an acquaintance of Callie's.

Who happens to be sitting next to my right foot, methodically licking her left hind leg.

When I walked out of the *Palmchat Gazette* offices, I was elated to find the cat on the hood of my red JEEP, which has become her customary spot. After morning greetings, I opened the door, then Callie jumped inside and settled onto the passenger seat.

"Where you heading, sis?" asked the cat.

"Dog park," I said.

"Why?" questioned the Calico. "You don't have a dog."

As I drove to the dog park, I explained to Callie why we were heading there.

"So ..." says the cat, rising to all fours. "Where's the dead body?"

"Let me ask Officer Cuetee and find out," I tell her.

In the past few months, as we've gotten to know each other, Officer Cuetee and I have met at the dog park several times to share information about various crimes. Normally, the dog park is crowded with excited canines running around and playing with each other as their humans sit on benches and relax.

At ten in the morning, following the discovery of a dead body, the park is a crime scene, festooned with yellow tape. A few canines and their worried-looking owners mill about in clusters around the perimeter of the chain link fence surrounding the enclosure. Also present are crime scene techs and a swarm of cops, including Officer Noah Cuetee, who spotted me when I entered the park.

I waved to him, and then he waved to me, and now he's walking over.

"Here comes Officer Good-looking," says Callie.

As he strides toward me, I take a moment to appreciate his good looks and tall, muscular frame. Officer Cuetee is a real dreamboat, as my grandma would say. Admittedly, I have kind of a quasi-crush on him, and I think he likes me, too, but we're not dating, or anything. We've gone out to dinner and we love to meet for tea and donuts. Occasionally, when Officer Cuetee has a weekend off, we go running. Well, he runs. I do a sort of jog-walk-shuffle and try my best to keep up. Anyway, so far, we've remained friends. And possibly, for right now, a friendship might be for the best, considering that I have to focus on my career. A whirlwind romance might be nice, but I can't allow myself the luxury of romantic distractions.

"Hey, Sophie," says Officer Cuetee, giving me a smile that showcases his adorable dimples.

"Hey," I say, smiling at him.

Glancing down at the Calico, Officer Cuetee says, "Hey, Callie."

"Girl, what did he say?" asked the cat.

"Callie, Officer Cuetee said hello," I tell her. "Can you say hello?"

The cat glances up at me. "Well, I could, but he won't understand me."

Officer Cuetee drops into a crouch to scratch Callie behind her ears, which she actually allows him to do.

Crossing my arms, I smirk at the cat, then say to Officer Cuetee, "Funny how she doesn't scratch your eyes out for touching her."

"Girl, don't hate," purrs the cat. "Officer Good-looking gives the best head scritches."

"Yeah, I'll bet he does," I tell the cat. "But I wouldn't know."

Standing, Officer Cuetee gives me a bemused look. "You bet I do but you wouldn't know what?"

Realizing my faux pas of talking to a cat and a human at the same time—which I seem to commit often, despite my best efforts—I clear my throat and ask, "So … how are you?"

"Despite the dead body in the dog park, doing good," he says, gesturing for me to follow him over toward a row of hibiscus bushes. "What about you?"

"Doing as well as I can be, I suppose, considering that, once again, I have to try to prove to my boss that I'm a good reporter," I say, trying not to sound so downtrodden. "So, I'm here to find out as much as I can about the dead body in the dog park."

Frowning, Officer Cuetee says, "How much proof does your boss need? Isn't it enough that you practically solved two murders? And both times you could have been killed."

"Apparently he needs more proof than that," I say, removing my phone from my crossbody purse. "And I am going to give it to him. So, if possible, can you share any detailed details with me? Anonymously, as always."

For the next ten minutes, as Callie continues to groom herself, Officer Cuetee gives me the lowdown.

Apparently, a few early morning risers were letting their dogs run around and play. Things were status quo until a quintet of canines congregating in a far corner of the park attracted the attention of their owners, who wondered what had entranced the dogs.

Turned out, the dogs were sniffing the dead body, which was on the other side of the fence, propped in a sitting position against the chain link. The dog owners hurried over and discovered a young woman stabbed to death.

"Any idea who the victim is?" I ask.

Nodding, Officer Cuetee says, "Her purse was found nearby. Inside, the identification in her wallet listed her as Annie Stone. We got the name from a California license."

"California?" I ask. "She's American?"

"Appears to be," says Officer Cuetee. "We confirmed that she arrived in the Palmchat Islands three months ago."

"A tourist?"

"Not exactly," says Officer Cuetee. "You're not going to believe this but ..."

"But ... what?"

Callie asks, "Girl, are you getting the detailed details? Because seems to me that you're asking a bunch of questions but not getting any answers."

"Well, I'm trying," I tell the cat.

"You're trying to ...what?" asks Officer Cuetee.

Clearing my throat, I say, "I'm trying to ... figure out what I'm not going to believe."

"Apparently, the victim works for a very famous celebrity," says Officer Cuetee, his Caribbean Sea blue eyes dancing with excitement. "Her passport was flagged as belonging to one of a group of VIP vacationers with special privileges and access. These visitors arrived on a private plane and were greeted by the Minister of Tourism."

"Who is the celebrity? Tell me, tell me," I insist, my mind whirring with ideas of who it might be. "Please tell me you aren't sworn to secrecy! I have to know!"

"A celebrity?" Callie jumps to all fours, arching her back. "Girl, who is it? Mr. Bigglesworth? Snowball? Choupette Lagerfeld?"

"Choupette Lagerfeld?" I echo, confused.

Laughing, Officer Cuetee asks, "Who is Choupette Lagerfeld?"

"Oh, um … " I give the cat a little scowl for distracting me, then focus on Officer Cuetee. "So, who's the celebrity?"

"Lucretia Lux."

I am flummoxed, and that's an understatement! Lucretia Lux is one of my favorite actresses. She's an A-list Oscar winner known as the Princess of Steampunk, which doesn't make much sense because most of her box office hits have been swoony romantic comedies. However, her first acting job was in a television show which reimagined Joan of Arc as an assassin who used 21st-century technology to take down the bad guys during the Crusades. An interesting premise, for sure, but I was never really into it. However, millions of people loved *Agent d'Arc*, and its steampunk elements.

"Lucretia Lux!" I let out a squeak, then gasp and slap a hand over my mouth.

"Lucretia Lux?" The cat settles into a loaf position. "Who is that?"

I let out another squeal. "Areyoukidding?"

"No, girl, I'm not kidding," says Callie. "Who is Lucretia Lux?"

Officer Cuetee frowns. "Huh?"

I drop my hand. "Are you kidding? Lucretia Lux is in St. Mateo? Ohmigoodness! I love Lucretia Lux. She's such a great actress. I adored her in *Stop in the Name of Love*! And *Before You Break My Heart*! And *Think it Over*!"

"Girl, I've never heard of any of those movies," says the Calico. "Are you sure she's a good actress?"

"Oh my goodness!" I squeak. "Wait!"

Officer Cuetee frowns. "What?"

"Lucretia Lux's assistant was murdered," I say. "How horrible! She must be devastated."

"We'll find out when she gets here," says Officer Cuetee.

"What? Wait!" I gasp, unable to contain my excitement. "Lucretia Lux is coming here? To the dog park?"

"She agreed to meet Detective François here and answer a few questions," says Officer Cuetee.

At the mention of the name Detective François, my excitement wanes.

Detective François is one of the famous five François brothers, a quintet of top-notch homicide detectives trained in the subtle art of crime investigation by none other than their grandfather, Sam François, the famed lawman responsible for capturing a notorious serial killer called The Fury.

Detective François is also intimidating and annoying, and not my biggest fan. Okay, to be honest, he's not a fan of me at all. And, full disclosure, it's not like I have any fans, so. Anyway, Detective François hates the press. He always refuses to give me a statement whenever I cover one of his murder investigations. Thus far, all I've gotten from him is a promise that he will never give me a comment.

"I'm surprised Lucretia Lux didn't want to meet Detective François privately in his office," I say, glancing over toward the group of dog owners and their hounds huddled between majestic Palm trees as they watch the cops and crime scene techs.

"I think Detective François would have preferred that," says Officer Cuetee, waving a hand to a trio of cops beckoning for him. "But, I heard—and this may just be a rumor—that she prefers to stay away from fluorescent lighting."

"I don't blame her," I say. "Fluorescent lights make your skin look terrible."

"Like you would know," says Officer Cuetee, giving me a sly, charming smile.

Charmed by his sly compliment, I feel my cheeks warm, but I refrain from giggling like a silly schoolgirl with a massive crush. Instead, I decide to maintain my professionalism, and say, "Well … um … yes … you see … that is …"

"Hey, I gotta get back to work," says Officer Cuetee, saving me from further embarrassment. "We'll talk later, okay."

Not trusting myself to speak, for fear that I'll open my mouth and out will come more ridiculous gibberish, I nod and wave.

As Officer Cuetee jogs back to the crime scene, I exhale. So much for my professionalism. Sheesh. Now do you see why I can't entertain any romantic dalliances? Anyway. I have witnesses to interview, per Marty's directives, and I intend to get the detailed details.

"Hey, what did Officer Good-looking say to make you get all dreamy-eyed?" asks the cat, rising to her feet.

Embarrassed, I say, "I wasn't dreamy-eyed."

"Girl, whatever," says Callie. "You were over the moon. Did he tell you that you were cute? Did he say he's sweet on you? Did he—"

"He didn't say any of that," I say, biting my lip, wondering how I would feel if Officer Cuetee did confess to having a crush on me.

"Maybe he didn't say it," says Callie. "But he was thinking it."

I glance down at the cat. "How would you know?"

"Girl, I told you," says Callie. "Cats know things."

Shaking my head, I say, "Well, here's what I know. I need details for my story, so …"

"I'll let you handle that, sis," says Callie. "I'll catch you later."

"Where are you going?"

"Wouldn't you like to know," sasses the cat, trotting away.

Chapter 3

Minutes later, as I head toward the group of dog owners and their canines, one of the pawrents strolls away from the others, trudging up the slope of grass.

I hurry off in her direction, hoping to intercept her.

Dressed in a blue jogging suit and sporting a matching baseball cap, she walks a small brown dog who wears a shirt the same color as her outfit.

"Excuse me? Ma'am ..." I say, stopping in front of her, halting her progress.

Frowning slightly, she slows, then bends down to scoop the little dog into her arms.

"Sorry to bother you," I say. "Do you have a moment?"

Taking a slight step back, she clutches the dog closer to her chest, causing the little canine to yelp.

"My name is Sophie Carter," I say, extending my hand. "I'm a reporter with the *Palmchat Gazette*."

Ignoring my hand, she says, "What is ... actually, I don't have a moment. Pinata needs to potty and he's allergic to grass so I have to take him to the public toilet."

"Pinata?" I ask, assuming she means the little brown dog, but something about what she said is confusing to me, though I'm not sure why.

"What is … my dog," she says.

Perplexed, I ask, "What is … your dog?"

"What is … Pinata."

"Um, I'm not sure I understand," I say. "What is … pinata?"

Exhaling, the woman says, "What is … my dog is Pinata."

"Oh, your dog is Pinata," I say. "The dog's name is Pinata."

Nodding, she says, "What is … yes."

"What is yes?" I ask, confused by her question, and wondering why she asked it. Nevertheless, I say, "Well, yes, is an answer in the affirmative."

The woman rolls her eyes. "What is … I know that."

"What is … you know what?"

Obviously frustrated, the woman shakes her head. "What is … I don't have time for this! Pinata has a weak bladder. I must get him to the toilet."

"Oh. Okay. Yes. Of course …" I stammer, but as she starts to walk away, I say, "But … before you go. Um. Is it just me or were you starting all of your sentences with the phrase … what is?"

"What is … yes, I was."

"Well, that explains it," I say, even though it doesn't. "Um … can I ask why?"

"What is … because I belong to the St. Mateo Canine Lovers' Jeopardy Appreciation Club."

"The St. Mateo Canine Lovers' Jeopardy Appreciation Club?"

"What is … that's right. And thus, whenever we meet, like we did this morning, we speak Jeopardy."

"Jeopardy?" I'm even more confused. "That's a language?"

"What is … it's a way of speaking. Everything we say must be in the form of a question, as per the rules of the television show, Jeopardy."

"Oh, now I get it," I say, then correct myself. "I mean ... what is ... oh, now I get it!"

The woman huffs at me, rolls her eyes again, and then stomps away.

Flabbergasted by the encounter, I glance toward the remaining pawrents, clustered near a tall, majestic Queen Palm. They're not just dog owners, I realize. They are also members of the St. Mateo Canine Lovers' Jeopardy Appreciation Club.

Which means, they're going to speak Jeopardy and answer all of my questions in the form of a question. Not exactly looking forward to that, but ...

I must get detailed details.

With that in mind, I take a deep breath and head over to the dog owners.

"Hi, folks! Don't mean to bother you," I begin, glancing at the dog-loving club members as they eye me with curiosity, suspicion, and aloofness. "My name is Sophie Carter. I'm a reporter from the *Palmchat Gazette* and I'd like to ask you a few questions if you have a moment."

The dog lovers glance at each other, saying nothing, making me wonder if they're communicating telepathically, or maybe—

"What is ... well, we've already given statements to the police, so why not," says a man holding the leash connected to a Doberman, sitting obediently at his side.

As the other dog owners shrug and nod, the dogs emit a few half-hearted, lazy barks.

Removing my phone from my cross body, I activate the recording app and ask, "Can you tell me who discovered the dead body?"

A man in a red T-shirt cradling a small dog in the crook of his arm says, "What is … Well, Alexander discovered the dead body, and—"

"What is … that is not true," interrupts an older man with hunched shoulders and gnarled hands, one of which grips a short leather leash attached to a hyperactive Scottish terrier. "Pineapple was the first to notice the dead body, weren't you boy, yes, you were, you saw the body first because you are so smart and observant and—"

"What is … that is a load of goatwash!" interjects a woman with a chihuahua in a baby carrier on her back. "First of all, Scottish terriers aren't that smart—"

"What is … I beg your pardon!" says the older man, nostrils flaring, revealing wiry nose hairs.

"What is … I'm sorry, but she's right," says the guy with the small dog.

The older man says, "What is … excuse me, but who asked you?"

"What is … all of you are wrong," says a woman with an English bulldog. "Bruno saw the body first."

"What is … Bruno is half blind!" The woman with the chihuahua declares. "There's no way he saw the dead body first!"

The English Bulldog's mom says, "What is … actually, he's half deaf!"

The woman with the chihuahua turns to me. "What is … actually, Chiquita saw the dead body first."

"What is … no, it was Disco!" says the man with the Doberman.

"What is … no, Alexander saw the body first and then the other dogs ran over," insists the man with the small dog.

"Guys, guys!" I shout. "You know what? That's okay …"

"What is … what do you mean?" demands the older man, scowling at me.

"What is … don't you want to know which dog really discovered the body first?" asks the man with the Doberman.

The small dog's dad says, "What is … we already know which dog discovered the body! It was—"

"What I meant was, I'll just ask Callie," I say, wishing I'd never approached the Jeopardy-loving dog pawrents.

"What is … who is Callie?" asks the chihuahua's mom.

"She's my cat," I say, then immediately correct myself. "Oops, sorry. Callie is not my cat. Don't tell her I said that. She'll scratch my eyes right out of my head. She's just a cat I know …"

The older man frowns. "What is … how is a cat going to tell you which dog discovered the dead body first?"

"Oh. Well. You see, um …" I trail off, kicking myself for a mistake I seem to make far too often—forgetting that I can't talk to people about Callie being able to talk to me because talking cats don't really exist even though Callie is a cat that talks to me.

At least, I think she's really talking to me.

Admittedly, sometimes, I'm not sure.

"What is … what's going on over there?" asks the man cradling the small dog, craning his neck to check out something behind me.

As the other pawrents look toward whatever has captured the small dog's dad's attention, I turn to see what's so fascinating.

About thirty feet away, several police officers form a half-circle around Detective François and the person he's talking to—a tall, slender woman dressed in chic white leggings and a tan-colored asymmetrical top with sun-kissed skin and buttery blonde hair cut in carefree waves. Even though she's wearing oversized black sunglasses, although there's no sun, I know who she is …

I gasp.

"What is … oh my God!"

"What is … is that who I think it is?"

"What is … that's—"

Lucretia Lux, I think, giddy with excitement as the canine pawrents pull out their phones and begin taking photos and videos. Lucretia Lux! Only thirty feet away from me. All I have to do is run up the sloping lawn, hop on the walking path, and muscle my way past the wall of cops, which seems to increase as more officers surround the detective and the A-list Oscar winner.

Hmmm, I think as I stealthily sidestep away from the pawrents, still star-struck by the Lucretia Lux sighting.

I have to talk to Ms. Lux. And not just because she's one of my favorite actresses and I want to ask for her autograph, which I absolutely want to do. But even more than that, I need to talk to Ms. Lux because the murder victim was her personal assistant. I have to get a comment from her. Even if it's no comment. Marty will absolutely expect it. And my article will absolutely go viral with a quote from Lucretia Lux. I could go viral, too. My story could get picked up by Good Morning Caribbean, Good Morning Britain, and Good Morning America. They might request a 30-second package with me where I'm interviewed by the hosts. I'll wear my tangerine wrap dress, which compliments my skin and gives me a jaunty, tropical vibe. And when they ask me to recount my experience interviewing Lucretia Lux, I'll tell them—

Two more cops join the half circle protecting Ms. Lux.

Shoot, I think, biting my lower lip. I'm never going to go viral and end up booking a segment on Good Morning Britain if I can't even get close to Ms. Lux so I can question her. Scanning the area, I spot a cluster of tall, thick Oleander bushes forming a natural privacy barrier behind Detective François and Lucretia Lux.

If I can make my way to the other side of the Oleander bushes, I can shimmy between them, and then I'll be within the semi-circle of cops and mere inches from Ms. Lux.

Confident in my plan, I head off ...

Chapter 4

Minutes later, I'm standing in the narrow space between two pink Oleander bushes, peeking through the leaves.

Staring at Lucretia Lux and Detective François, I feel a thrill of excitement. Ms. Lux and the lawman are about a foot away from me, and they have no idea that I'm hiding in the trees listening. Part of me feels like a Palmchat Islands Investigative Bureau superspy. And another part of me feels a tad sketchy and lowkey borderline stalkerish. But, I do plan to make my presence known. When Detective François completes his questioning, of course. Despite Marty's insistence that I get a quote from the irritable, irascible detective, I'm not going to bother.

"I assure you, Ms. Lux," says Detective François. "I intend to find out what happened to your assistant."

"Detective François," begins Ms. Lux. "I have no doubt you will discover the killer fairly quickly. I just want my dog found."

"Your dog?" deadpans Detective François.

Lucretia Lux says, "His name is James Mortimer."

"James Mortimer?" asks Detective François.

"When your officers informed me that my assistant had been

killed, and they didn't mention that my dog had been left behind," says Ms. Lux, "I knew he was missing. Someone took him. Kidnapped him. I'd like you to find him."

Shocked and riveted and worried, I nevertheless summon the presence of mind to take out my phone and activate my recording app. As quietly as possible, I take a step forward, trying to get closer without exposing myself.

"Why do you think your dog would have been left behind after your assistant was murdered?" asks Detective François.

"Because my assistant took my dog out last night," says Ms. Lux. "To this dog park."

"Why would your assistant take your dog to the dog park at night?" asks François.

"I instructed her not to take James Mortimer to the dog park during the day," says Ms. Lux. "There would be too many people around. Lots of paparazzi."

Nodding, the detective asks, "What kind of dog is it?"

I wonder the same thing, wriggling my right foot, which itches a bit, particularly around the ankle.

"He's a purebred Corgi," says Lucretia Lux. "I'd like him found as soon as possible."

I know exactly how she feels. When Callie was kidnapped, I was beside myself with grief and worry, even though Callie is fiercely independent and can take care of herself and isn't even my cat. None of that mattered when the feisty Calico was missing. All I could focus on was finding her.

"If you want your dog found, you need to go down to the station," says Detective François, "and report your dog stolen. After you give an official statement about the death of your assistant and answer any more questions I may have."

Detective François doesn't seem that interested in finding the missing dog, I think, reaching down to scratch my ankle. But maybe—

My fingers skim across something that feels cold, scaly, and rubbery. Hmmm. Maybe I need to exfoliate. And moisturize. I glance at my ankle. A thin grass snake slithers around my ankle. Screaming, I kick my foot out and up, desperate to get the snake off me. The snake flies up in the air. Fearing it might land on me, I crash through the Oleander bushes, trying to get away and slam into a brick wall.

The wind knocked from me, I gasp as I stumble and fall back, landing on my backside in the grass.

"Ms. Carter …"

Trying to catch my breath, I glance up at the brick wall—Detective François.

"Ummm …" I say, mortified, glancing around at the officers staring at me, their expressions a mix of confusion, amusement, derision, and apathy. Only Officer Cuetee looks concerned as he steps forward to help me to my feet.

"You okay, Sophie?" asks Officer Cuetee, voice lowered.

"Yeah, I'm fine," I whisper back. "I just—"

"Were you in that Oleander bush, Ms. Carter?" demands Detective François.

Cringing, I turn to the detective, whose scowl doesn't detract from his brooding good looks. "Well, um, you see, I … um—"

"Well, um, I see, you … um … what?"

"Well …" I clear my throat, embarrassed by the officers staring at me, and intimidated by Detective François's grim scowl. "I was just hoping to get a comment from you."

This, of course, is not true. I am totally not hoping for a comment from him, because it's hopeless, and he's only going to tell me—

"No comment, Ms. Carter," growls François. "I've already told you, I will never have any comments for any of your stories, so—"

"You have no comment for her stories?" interjects Ms. Lux,

looking from the detective to me, and then back to the detective. "What stories?"

"He means my article," I say.

Ms. Lux asks, "What article?"

I say, "The article I'm going to write about the dead body found at the dog park, who happens to be your assistant, and may I say, Ms. Lux, that I'm sorry for your loss, and also, you are one of my favorite actresses!"

"Thank you, I appreciate that," says Ms. Lux.

Detective François clears his throat. "I need to head back to the station and you should follow me, Ms. Lux, so you can give me that official statement."

"And I have to report that James Mortimer was taken," says Ms. Lux.

"Yeah, that, too," mumbles Detective François, turning from her, and motioning for several of the officers to follow him.

"I'm right behind you," says Ms. Lux waving at the detective before turning to me. "About this article you're writing. Are you a reporter?"

Smiling, I check my recording app and say, "Yes, as a matter of fact, I am! My name is Sophie Carter, and I'm an investigative reporter at the *Palmchat Gazette*. I'm hoping you'll give me a comment about your assistant's death. You could tell me how you feel, and if you have any suspects I should investigate, or—"

"Well, actually," says Ms. Lux, "I was hoping you might do a story on the kidnapping of James Mortimer."

Slightly confused, I ask, "You want me to write an article about your missing dog?"

I don't want to disappoint her, but I doubt Marty will consent to an in-depth piece about a purloined canine, especially since there's no evidence that the Corgi was taken.

"I'm thinking that he'll be found quickly if people know he's missing," says Ms. Lux.

I take a quick breath. "Ms. Lux, listen, I totally feel your pain about your missing dog because my cat was missing ... wait, I don't mean that *my* cat was missing because I don't have a cat ... but there's this cat I know, and we're super close ... well, wait, I consider myself close to her, but I'm not quite sure if—"

"You'll need photos of James Mortimer for the story," says Ms. Lux.

Not quite sure she heard me, I say, "You see, actually ..."

Ms. Lux pulls a mini walkie-talkie from beneath her oversized shirt and brings it to her mouth. "Esteban? Where are you?"

I frown. "Esteban?"

"My driver," she explains. "He has lots of photos of James Mortimer on his phone."

"Ms. Lux ..."

Startled by the voice, I turn toward the right.

Walking along the path is a young, somewhat muscular guy of medium height wearing tan pants and a tropical shirt with flowers and toucan birds printed on it. He holds a mini walkie-talkie in one hand and a phone in the other.

"James Mortimer is missing," says Ms. Lux.

"Oh my God," says Esteban.

Her expression pained, Ms. Lux glances at me. "This is Sophie Carter with the *Palmchat Gazette*. She's going to write a story about James Mortimer's disappearance."

I clear my throat. "Well, actually—"

"We'll need a photo of James Mortimer," says Ms. Lux, focusing on her driver. "You have some pictures of him on your phone, right?"

"I should," says Esteban.

"Great," says Ms. Lux. "I'm going to step over here and make some phone calls. Can you give Ms. Carter the photo of James Mortimer and my contact information?"

Nodding, Esteban says, "Will do."

Removing her phone, Lucretia Lux walks to the line of hibiscus bushes, several feet from me and her driver, who I turn to and say, "Listen, I'm not sure—"

"I'll send over a photo later," says Esteban, pulling a sticky pad and pen from his pocket. "I don't have any of Ms. Lux's business cards, but I can write her contact info down for you."

"Right," I say, frowning. "But, you see—"

"What's your number?"

After giving it to him, I say, "I need to tell you that—"

"Esteban?" calls Ms. Lux. "We need to get down to the police station."

Nodding at his boss, Esteban tears the top square from the sticky pad and hands it to me. "Call if you need any information about James Mortimer for your article. I'll text you a pic."

"Yes, okay, but—"

Esteban turns and hurries away.

Chapter 5

Confused and glum, despite the hint of sun peeking through the low deck of rumbling, charcoal clouds, I stare at the sheet from the sticky pad Lucretia Lux's driver gave me.

On the blush pink colored paper, the following is written in somewhat regal, slanted block letters:

> LUCRETIA L. LUX
> 2 GOLDEN GRAVEL WAY
> ST. MATEO, PALMCHAT ISLANDS

Biting my lip, I grab my cross-body purse from the passenger seat and exit the JEEP. It's almost noon, and instead of figuring out what I might want for lunch, I'm back at work, having just parked in the *Palmchat Gazette* parking lot.

Marty sent me to get the detailed details about the dead body found in the dog park. That's what he wants me to write about. He is not going to be pleased when I relay that Lucretia Lux asked me to write a story about James Mortimer's kidnapping. If, in fact, James

Mortimer was actually dognapped. It is quite possible, that after Ms. Lux's assistant was tragically stabbed to death, the purebred Corgi fled the scene in shock and terror.

I don't even have enough detailed details about James Mortimer, or his alleged dognapping, to write an article about the missing canine. And again, Marty is not going to let me write about the missing dog of an A-list actress. And, again, as my grandma would say, that goat ain't gonna hunt. Not that goats hunt, but you know what I mean ...

Anyhoo, thinking about the dead body found in the dog park, I need to get to my desk and transcribe the recordings I made. The Jeopardy-obsessed dog lovers didn't have much information about the dead body, but I think I got enough details from Officer Cuetee to come up with a first draft for Marty. So—

"Hey girl, hey ..."

Recognizing the sassy tone, I smile and glance to my right, where Callie the Calico sits on the hood of my JEEP, licking her fur.

"Callie! Hey! How are you?" I'm happy to see the cat, and I'd love to grab her and cuddle her, but I know she would curve me, so I give her an enthusiastic wave with both hands. "Where have you been? Seems like I haven't seen you in ages!"

"Girl, you saw me two hours ago," says Callie, staring at me.

"Yeah, I guess I did," I say, leaning against the JEEP.

"So, what happened after I left?" asks Callie. "Did you get the detailed details?"

Shaking my head, I wave the sticky note. "I got this."

"What's that?" asks Callie.

"Lucretia Lux's contact information," I say, folding the sticky note in half and shoving it to the bottom of my cross-body.

"So you met the actress?"

I glance at the sticky pad sheet again. "Yeah ..."

"Girl, you don't sound happy about it," says Callie, licking her paw. "I thought she was your favorite actress."

"She is, but ..."

"But what?" asks Callie. "She tried to act snobby and snooty with you, didn't she? Girl, I'm not surprised. Actresses are whiny, bratty divas. Reminds me of my friend Tori. She's a Tortoiseshell cat and she starred in cat food commercials when she was a kitten. You couldn't tell her anything. She thought she was the cat's meow. Pun intended."

"So, you met an actress, too?" I ask. "When was this?"

"It was when ... " Callie trails off and looks away.

"When ...?" I prompt.

"Girl, it doesn't matter," says the cat dismissively.

At once, I could kick myself. It's not that it doesn't matter. It's that Callie doesn't remember when she met Tori, even though she remembers Tori. Because of the selective catnesia. According to Callie, it affects her the same way selective amnesia affects humans. Some things you remember. Other things you can't recall. And you don't know why. There's no rhyme or reason.

The selective catnesia reminds me of my promise to Callie.

I'm supposed to contact her real owners so she can return to them. Callie has pawrents, but she doesn't remember them. Her real humans are probably looking for her, wondering what happened to her. Hoping she'll come back to them.

"What does the bratty diva actress want you to do?" asks Callie.

Sighing, I say, "Actually, she's not a bratty diva actress. She was so super nice, considering that her dog is missing."

"I didn't ask you if she was nice, sis," says the Calico. "I asked what she wants you to do."

"She wants me to write an article about her missing dog."

"Girl, you don't work for *Dog Fancy* magazine," says Callie. "You're a reporter for the *Palmchat Gazette*."

"Anyway," I say. "I have the Herculean task of convincing Marty to let me cover the dognapping even though he wants me to do a story about the dead body found in the dog park."

"Then you need to write about the dead body found in the dog park," advises Callie.

"But what about the dognapping," I say, biting my lip.

"Girl, you can't be worried about a missing canine," says Callie. "You need to think about your career. Sis, did you forget that your boss wants to ship you out? Don't give him a good excuse to fire you."

"I know, but, Ms. Lux really wants me to write an article about her missing dog."

"Sis, Ms. Lux is not the boss of you," says the feisty feline.

"I know that," I say. "But, she is—or was—the boss of Annie Stone, the woman who was stabbed to death at the dog park. It kind of just occurred to me that if I find James Mortimer, Ms. Lux will be so grateful that she'll give me an exclusive interview about the death of her assistant."

"You're probably right," agrees the cat. "Still you can't lose your job. So, I'll see what I can find out about the dog. You focus on the dead body at the dog park."

"Oh, Callie, thank you so much!" I gush, restraining myself from reaching out to scratch the cat behind her ear. I know better.

"Don't mention it," says the cat as she leaps from the hood of the JEEP down to the concrete. "On second thought … mention it, sis. Often."

Laughing, I watch Callie trot away.

Thirty minutes later, I'm at my cubicle, thinking of how I want to start the first draft of my article about the dead body in the dog park when my desk phone rings.

Honestly, I'm thankful for the interruption because I really have no idea how to start the story. And I don't think I have enough detailed details to write it. And I'm not sure the peppermint tea helped, which makes me wonder if I chose the wrong flavor of tea. Does peppermint help my writing? Or, is it mango blueberry? Or guava blackberry? Or maybe it's—

The shrill ringing arrests my attention.

I grab the phone, and answer it with a cheery, *"Palmchat Gazette,* Sophie Carter speaking. How can I help you?"

"Hey, Sophie, it's Noah," says Officer Cuetee.

"Hey, how are you?"

"I don't have a lot of time to talk," he says. "But, I wanted to tell you there's been a break in the dog park murder. François arrested a suspect."

Grabbing a pen and a yellow legal pad, I say, "Already? Who is it?"

"Lucretia Lux's chef," says Officer Cuetee.

"The chef killed the assistant?" I ask, scribbling notes I hope I'll be able to read after I hang up with Officer Cuetee.

"That's what François thinks," says Officer Cuetee. "We found the murder weapon behind a hibiscus bush. A kitchen knife with the chef's prints on it. Turns out, the chef has a record so when forensic ran the prints, her name came up."

"The chef is a woman?"

"Her name is Bonnie Lambeaux," he says. "And the knife had her initials carved on the hilt. It definitely belonged to her and she was the only one who used it. None of the other staff prepared meals for Ms. Lux."

"The chef kill the assistant in the park with the knife?" I ask. "Is there a motive?"

"Glad you asked," he tells me. "After Bonnie Lambeaux was arrested, her cell phone was confiscated. Lots of incriminating texts between Bonnie and Annie Stone, including a text where the chef agreed to meet the assistant at the dog park last night. They were going to talk about money the chef was going to give Annie."

"Why was the chef going to give the assistant money?" I ask.

"Apparently," says Officer Cuetee. "The assistant was blackmailing the chef ..."

Chapter 6

The next morning, Marty buzzes my desk phone.

"Come to my office," grumbles Marty. "We need to discuss the dog park murder."

With bright cheer in my tone, I say, "Absolutely, I'll be right—"

Marty hangs up.

As I disconnect the line on my end, I realize I could be disheartened and miffed, but there's no reason for melancholy. Eight in the morning is much too early for self-pity, and besides, I've already had a steaming mug of lavender tea with sugarplum donut holes. Thus, I am ready to face whatever feedback Marty wants to give me on my dog park murder article.

Yesterday, after Officer Cuetee provided me with additional detailed details, I was able to write a first draft. CHEF STABS ASSISTANT AT DOG PARK. Not to toot my own horn, but my story was an enthralling narrative featuring a homicidal chef with evidence stacked against her and a shady assistant who was also a secret extortionist.

Moments later, I enter Marty's office.

"Sit down," he orders.

After I comply, I ask, "What did you think of my story?"

"Wasn't as bad as I thought it would be," says Marty. "But it wasn't as good as it should have been, considering that you actually met Lucretia Lux."

"Yes, I did!"

"So why didn't you get a comment from her when you found out that her chef killed her assistant?" asks Marty. "You should have asked her about the assistant blackmailing the chef? Did she know about that?"

"Well, I talked to Ms. Lux before I found out that her chef killed her assistant—"

"And did she have any idea who might have killed her assistant? I didn't see that in your story. Did you ask her that?"

"Well, yes, you see, um … I asked her that, but she didn't answer me because she was so upset about James Mortimer."

"James Mortimer?"

"Her dog," I say. "He's a purebred Corgi, and he is missing."

"What does her missing dog have to do with her dead assistant?"

"You know, I'm glad you asked that," I say, "because as it turns out, the assistant took the Corgi to the dog park last night. The assistant had the dog when she was killed by the chef—"

"Allegedly," interjects Marty.

"Absolutely," I agree, then say, "So, anyway, honestly, I'm not sure the Corgi was dognapped. He might have run off when the assistant was murdered—allegedly—by the chef."

"But Ms. Lux thinks the Corgi was kidnapped?"

Nodding, I say, "And she wants me to write about the missing dog, but I'm going to focus on the dog park murder and Callie will see what she can find out about the dog."

Marty frowns. "Callie?"

"Just this cat I know," I say, thankful that I didn't accidentally refer to Callie as my cat, as I'm prone to accidentally do.

"A cat you know? Wait. Are you talking about the same cat who attacked you and you ended up in the hospital?"

Nodding, I say, "Same cat."

Giving me a skeptical, shrewd look, Marty folds his arms across his barrel chest. "And how is this cat that you know going to find out what happened to the missing dog?"

"Well, yes, you see, um ... " I clear my throat. "What I meant was, I think maybe I should write an article about the dognapping because the story would absolutely trend, which would be great for the paper, and it would give me more access to Ms. Lux, and while she's providing information about the dog, I can ask her about her dead assistant ... and I can talk to the rest of the staff. What do you think?

Marty's eyes narrow. "I think I can't believe you thought of that ..."

I think I've just been insulted, but I'm not quite sure, so ...

"Anyway, I need a follow-up to the dog park murder story," says Marty, leaning back in his creaky leather chair. "I've arranged a jailhouse interview with the chef, Bonnie Lambeaux. Find out what she has to say for herself other than she's innocent and didn't do it."

"Got it," I say.

"Then, contact Ms. Lux," says Marty. "Tell her you need additional information for the dognapping story and then question her about the assistant's murder and the chef's arrest."

"Absolutely!"

"And don't blow it, Sophia," warns Marty.

Chapter 7

"As I told the police, Annie was blackmailing me, yes, that's true," says Lucretia Lux's chef, Bonnie Lambeaux, who looks surprisingly chic and glamourous despite her surroundings. She's got the looks of a centerfold, with glossy auburn hair, bright, clear skin, great cheekbones, and a beauty mole to the left of her pouty mouth.

"And you texted Annie to meet you at the dog park?" I ask, recalling the details Officer Cuetee gave me.

Tossing her shampoo commercial mane, Chef Bonnie says, "Yes, that's true. I texted Annie and set up the meeting at the dog park to pay her the blackmail money."

"Why'd you choose the dog park?"

"Well, I knew it would be deserted at midnight," says Chef Bonnie. "I also knew that Annie took James Mortimer to the dog park every night. I figured it would be the perfect place. Very private and no paps."

"Paps?" I ask, unfamiliar with the word.

"Paparazzi," clarifies Chef Bonnie. "They found out that Ms. Lux bought a vacation home in St. Mateo three months ago, and some of them flew to the island and set up camp, hoping to get photos of her.

Some of them want pics of the dog, too. James Mortimer is very popular. He has a large social media following."

Making a mental note to check out the Corgi's socials, I ask, "So, what happened when you met Annie and James Mortimer at the dog park?"

"I didn't meet Annie at the dog park," says Chef Bonnie. "I was supposed to, but I didn't show up because I didn't have the money. I thought I would be able to borrow it from a friend, but that didn't happen, so ..."

"So, while Annie was waiting for you to show up, where were you?"

Bonnie tosses her hair again, then sighs. "I was walking along the boardwalk in Guavatown, trying to think of what to do. I ended up sitting down on a bench and falling asleep. Of course, because I was alone, I can't prove that."

"So, you have no alibi?"

Shaking her head, Chef Bonnie says, "Unfortunately, no. So, the cops don't believe my story. They think I killed Annie, but that's not true. I mean, yes, it's true that Annie deserved to die ..."

"She did?"

"Annie was a greedy, heartless sea hag," declares Chef Bonnie. "She took every last cent I had. She even took money from me that I didn't have. She even took all of my jewelry. That soulless banshee took the clothes off my back. But I didn't kill her."

"The fact that Annie was blackmailing you gives you a very strong motive for murder," I tell her.

"Yes, that's true," acknowledges Chef Bonnie with another head toss.

"Why was she blackmailing you?"

Sighing, Chef Bonnie says, "She found out that I was borrowing some of Ms. Lux's purses and a few of her other valuables, and I was selling them on the black market."

"So Annie threatened to tell Ms. Lux that you were stealing—"

"Borrowing," interjects Chef Bonnie.

"But if you sold the purses and other valuables, how could you return them to Ms. Lux."

"I hadn't quite worked that out," admits Chef Bonnie. "But I didn't steal anything. Thieves don't borrow. Thieves take with no intention of giving back. I, on the other hand, intended to return the items I borrowed, which I explained to Annie. But she said Ms. Lux wouldn't see it that way. Ms. Lux would think I'd stolen from her, even though I didn't, but I knew Annie was right."

Nodding, even though I don't understand her faulty logic, I say, "Okay, well ... the cops have other damaging evidence against you. Namely the kitchen knife with your prints on it that was found in some hibiscus bushes at the dog park."

"Yes, that's true, as well," says Chef Bonnie. "But if I had killed Annie, do you think I would have used one of my good knives? I have to chop vegetables with that knife! I wouldn't use it to stab anybody. Especially not her. That knife is too good to stab her with. If I was going to stab her, I would use a cheap paring knife."

"How do you explain that your knife was found in the dog park?" I ask.

"Someone must have stolen my knife," she says. "That's what I told the cops. I'm being framed!"

"Who would do that?"

Chef Bonnie sneers, tosses her hair and rolls her eyes. "Obviously, the person who killed Annie is framing me."

"What I mean is," I say, "who do you think is framing you? Who do you think killed Annie?"

"I don't think," says Chef Bonnie. "I know who killed Annie Stone."

"You do?"

"It was Lucretia Lux."

Though I'm doubtful, I don't want to assume that the chef is lying. "Lucretia Lux killed her assistant?" Chef Bonnie nods. "That's why she's willing to let me rot in this cell. I called Ms. Lux and asked her to bail me out, but she refused. Can you believe that? After all the food I've cooked for her. After all the vegetables I've sliced, diced, and julienned for her. After the eggs I've poached. After the asparagus I've blanched. After the black beans and sweet potatoes I've pureed into soup, even after the immersion blender broke!"

"You made black bean and sweet potato soup by hand?" I ask, impressed.

"All I had was a mortal, a pestle, and a wire whisk that had seen much better days," says Chef Bonnie. "I garnished it with cojita cheese crumbles and fresh avocado."

"Sounds delicious," I say, remembering that I haven't had lunch.

Chef Bonnie tsks. "Ms. Lux complained that the avocado was cut too thin. Anyway, she refused to bail me out. Why? Because she killed Annie Stone but she wants me to go to prison for a crime she committed!"

"Why would Ms. Lux kill her assistant?"

"Annie was also blackmailing Ms. Lux," says Chef Bonnie. "A couple of months ago, Ms. Lux kicked James Mortimer."

Shocked, I gasp. "Ms. Lux kicked her own dog? Are you serious? Why? She seems crazy about that dog!"

"She is crazy about him," says the chef. "Ms. Lux didn't kick him on purpose. She was startled by a turtle."

"A turtle?"

"There are dozens of them out in the lake behind the house," explains the chef. "They're a nuisance. Only good for turtle soup. Anyway, they always seem to find their way onto the terrace. Well, one day, Ms. Lux was frightened when she saw something moving beneath a beach towel. She thought it was a turtle, but it was James

Mortimer, hiding beneath the towel. And she kicked what she thought was the turtle beneath the towel across the terrace."

"Oh my goodness!" I exclaim.

"Ms. Lux bent it like Beckham," says the chef. "Immediately, James Mortimer began yelping as he crawled from beneath the towel. Ms. Lux was destroyed. She couldn't apologize enough to the dog. She had to call the vet. James Mortimer had two bone fractures."

"Oh, no," I say, empathizing with Ms. Lux's worry for her animal as I recall Callie's leg injury, which she staunchly refused to have the vet check out until she could barely walk and had no choice.

"Anyway, the injury to James Mortimer was an accident," says the chef. "But, Annie Stone stole the interior surveillance camera footage and edited it so that it appears Ms. Lux intentionally kicked the poor mutt."

Shaking my head, I say, "If the public saw that camera footage—"

"Ms. Lux would be destroyed. Canceled. Vilified across each and every social media platform," says the chef. "Her career would be finished. She would lose each and every one of her endorsements, brand deals, and sponsorships. Annie Stone knew that and she was forcing Ms. Lux to pay for her silence. But Ms. Lux was getting sick and tired of Annie's blackmail."

"And so you think Ms. Lux killed Annie Stone," I say, considering the theory.

"I know she did," insists the chef.

"But, you know the same thing can be said about you," I point out. "Annie Stone was blackmailing you, too. Maybe you got sick and tired of the blackmail and killed Annie."

Bonnie shakes her glossy mane. "But, I didn't. Like I said, I'm being framed by the person who killed Annie Stone—Lucretia Lux."

Chapter 8

"What questions do you have about James Mortimer for the article about his disappearance?" asks Lucretia Lux as she takes a seat on a plush, oversized sectional couch.

At the moment, we're on the large terrace of her fabulous beachfront villa. Although it does occur to me that the terrace, as fabulous as it is, might be more tremendous if it actually faced the gorgeous stretch of white sand beach that borders the front of the palatial estate. Instead, the terrace faces a large pool, beyond which is a large lake, and beyond that is a dense grove of mango and banana trees.

After my jailhouse interview with Chef Bonnie, I contacted Ms. Lux using the private phone number the chef gave me. I explained that I was seeking additional information about James Mortimer, and had other questions also, and she agreed to see me.

"Well, yes, you see, I … um … " I clear my throat to stall for time. And to ponder how I'm going to bring up Chef Bonnie Lambeaux's accusation against Ms. Lux—that the A-list actress killed Annie Stone because the assistant was blackmailing her. Although, I suppose the best way to question Ms. Lux is to just be direct and to the point. But

I don't want to start things out with a confrontational tone. I want to be sly and subtle with my interrogation. I want to cleverly trick Ms. Lux into incriminating herself and confessing the truth. If, in fact, the chef was being honest and the truth is that Ms. Lux killed Annie Stone.

"Ms. Lux, before we discuss James Mortimer's dognapping," I begin, "I'd like to ask you—"

"What is there to discuss other than James Mortimer's dognapping?" Ms. Lux frowns.

"Your assistant, Annie Stone," I say. "Do you have any idea who might have killed her?"

Ms. Lux stares at me, and for a moment, I wonder if she didn't understand my question, but then she glances away and says, "I know exactly who killed Annie. And so do the police. It was my former chef, Bonnie Lambeaux."

"Former chef?"

Her expression pained, Ms. Lux says, "Obviously, when she was arrested, I had no choice but to terminate her employment, effective immediately. I will not have a murderer on my payroll."

"Why are you so sure that Bonnie killed Annie?"

Ms. Lux gives me an irritated look. "Because Annie was blackmailing Bonnie. Obviously, I had no idea, but Detective François shared with me that Annie and Bonnie arranged to meet the night Annie was murdered. Bonnie killed Annie because she couldn't keep making the extortion payments."

"Bonnie does have a strong motive for murder," I agree.

"Bonnie has more than a strong motive," says Ms. Lux. "One of her knives—the murder weapon—was found at the scene of the crime. And she doesn't have an alibi."

"That's true, but—"

"It gives me chills to think that a killer was living under my roof," says Ms. Lux, shivering. "A killer who was also a thief, according to

Detective François. He told me that Bonnie had been stealing from me and selling the items on the Internet."

"Right, but—"

"Ms. Lux …"

At the sound of the deep voice, I glance over my shoulder.

Esteban, Ms. Lux's driver, strides toward the couch. "Your manager needs to speak with you. The Skype call is set up in your office."

"Thanks so much, Esteban," says Ms. Lux, standing. Turning to me, she says, "I'm afraid we have to cut this short. I don't know how long this call will take. Esteban can answer your questions about James Mortimer."

After watching Ms. Lux walk away, I pivot to face Esteban.

But the driver is distracted, staring at the ground. "How do these turtles keep getting onto the terrace?"

Following Esteban's gaze, I spot the small turtles. Three of them, to be exact, slowly making their way across the travertine tile.

At once, I'm reminded of Bonnie's story about Ms. Lux kicking the turtle, which was hiding beneath the beach towel, which turned out not to be a turtle but her beloved Corgi. Supposedly, Annie Stone was blackmailing Ms. Lux about accidentally kicking the dog, so Ms. Lux killed her. An interesting theory I didn't get a chance to ask Ms. Lux about, unfortunately.

"So, you have questions about James Mortimer?" asks Esteban as he bends down to scoop up the first turtle, which he places in the crook of his arm.

"Actually … I just need the photo of the dog for my article," I say. "You never sent it to me. And you didn't give me a number to call you."

"Oh, I lost your number. " Esteban hurries across the terrace to grab the second turtle before it heads beneath the couch. "By the way, make sure you mention that James Mortimer was gifted to Ms.

Lux by the King of England himself when Ms. Lux was invited to Buckingham Palace."

Somewhat impressed, I say, "Are you serious?"

Frowning, Esteban glances around the terrace. "The king is a huge fan of *Agent D'Arc*."

I'm astonished. "Really?"

Nodding, Esteban stalks slowly back and forth across the terrace. "Anyway, I'll send a good photo of James Mortimer. Just leave your email information on the table in the foyer."

"Before I go," I say. "Can I ask you a few questions about Annie's murder?"

"Help me find this last turtle and you can ask me whatever you want," says Esteban, peering behind a large stone flowerpot.

"It's a deal," I say, strolling over to the couch, which has about eight accent pillows stacked in front of the back cushions. Starting my search, I pick up a pillow. No turtle hiding there, but I have seven more to go, so there is hope. "So ... do you think Bonnie killed Annie?"

"I'm not sure," says Esteban. "But, I certainly hope not. Don't like thinking that I've been working with a homicidal maniac for the past six months."

I pick up the third pillow. Still no turtle. "Well, the cops say Bonnie has a compelling motive. Apparently, Annie was blackmailing Bonnie. Did you know about that?"

"Ms. Lux said the cops told her that," says Esteban, dropping to one knee to peek under a large cane chair. "But I'm not sure I believe it. Bonnie and Annie were always friendly to each other, from what I saw."

"Which means there were probably times when you didn't see them being friendly to each other," I point out. "Maybe there were times when they were being mean to each other but you didn't see it."

Shrugging as he checks under a side table, Esteban says, "Yeah, I suppose. Man, where is that last turtle?"

I pick up the fourth pillow. "Well, he's not hiding beneath any of the pillows I've checked under so far."

Exhaling, his face a mask of frustration, Esteban says, "Ms. Lux will go ballistic if she sees another turtle on this terrace. And if one ever gets into the house, she'll kill me."

Struck by his turn of phrase, I ask, "Does Ms. Lux get homicidal about things often?"

Esteban frowns at me. "Ms. Lux is not homicidal."

"You said she would kill you if a turtle got in the house."

The driver scowls. "I didn't mean that ..."

"Listen, I have to ask ..." I start. "Do you think Ms. Lux could have killed Annie?"

Esteban looks at me like I have two heads. Possibly three. "What? Ms. Lux? Kill Annie? Are you serious? No way. Never. Not. A. Chance."

"Did you know that Annie Stone was blackmailing Ms. Lux?"

"Why would Annie blackmail Ms. Lux?" asks the driver.

"Ms. Lux kicked James Mortimer," I say.

Esteban shakes his head. "That was an accident. She mistook the dog for a turtle."

"Right," I say. "And then Annie stole the camera footage and edited it so it looks like Ms. Lux kicked the dog on purpose."

"Who told you that?"

"Bonnie Lambeaux."

"Bonnie's lying," says Esteban.

"How can you be so sure?"

"Look, Bonnie has been arrested for murder," says Esteban. "She'll say anything to get out of jail. Even something as ridiculous as Ms. Lux killing Annie. But, Ms. Lux didn't want Annie dead."

"At least you don't think she did," I point out. "But if Bonnie is telling the truth, then Ms. Lux would have a strong motive. She wouldn't want the world to see footage of her kicking James Mortimer."

"Ms. Lux didn't kick the dog on purpose and Annie knew that," says Esteban. "She wouldn't blackmail Ms. Lux. And, as I said, I don't know if I believe that Annie was blackmailing Bonnie, either."

I check under the remaining pillows as Esteban makes a few more circles around the terrace. "Okay, then, who do you think killed Annie?"

"I have no idea," says Esteban. "Annie was a sweet girl. I can't believe anybody wanted to kill her."

"And yet Annie was stabbed to death," I say. "With Bonnie's knife."

"Yeah, that's kind of weird," says Esteban. "But, look, I really need to find the last turtle. So, all I can think is that Annie wasn't the intended target."

Intrigued by his theory, I ask, "So you don't think Annie was supposed to be killed?"

Shaking his head, Esteban says, "I think she was killed because of James Mortimer. I think he was dognapped on purpose. Annie died protecting the dog. If the cops find the dognapper, then they'll find the person who killed Annie."

"Interesting," I say. And it is. But it still begs the question of why the dognapper would use Bonnie's knife to kill Annie. And how could the dognapper have gotten Bonnie's knife?

"Problem is, the cops aren't interested in finding the dog," says Esteban. "Which is why Ms. Lux wants you to do the article on James Mortimer. And speaking of that, don't forget to leave your email information on the table in the foyer on your way out. I'll send you a photo."

Chapter 9

An hour later, I'm back at the *Palmchat Gazette* offices, sitting at the desk in my cubicle.

Naturally, I should be organizing notes for my follow-up dog park murder article, which will feature the jailhouse interview with Bonnie and highlights from the beach house interviews with Ms. Lux and Esteban, but instead, I'm contemplating what I'd like to have for lunch.

It's been a very eventful morning.

I'm beyond famished.

But I'm not sure what I'm in the mood for. Do I want curried goat and rice? Or goat empanadas with stewed plantains? Or maybe—

My desk phone buzzes.

I answer, "This is—"

"Sophia, come to my office now," orders Marty.

"Absolutely! I'll be right there," I promise. "Should I bring a—"

The line goes dead.

Jumping up, I grab my oversized bag since I plan on heading out for lunch following the meeting and stroll to Marty's office. Five minutes later, my boss points at the chair in front of his desk and says, "Sit."

Only slightly worried, I take a seat. Marty is pacing back and forth behind his desk, and he's scowling, and his face is fire ant red, but he's always pacing and scowling and red-faced. He might be upset with me about something. After all, he usually is. But, then again, he might not.

"Your dog park murder story is performing better than expected," says Marty, as though it pains him to do so. "Therefore, I need the first draft of the follow-up on my desk before you leave."

"Absolutely!" I say, overjoyed that my article is doing well.

"Sophia, this goes without saying but it bears repeating," begins Marty. "You can't drop the ball on this follow-up."

"I absolutely will not drop the ball," I promise. "You can count on me."

"How did the jailhouse interview go?"

"Great!" I say. "I got lots of detailed details."

"You think the chef killed the assistant?"

"I'm not sure," I say. "The evidence against her is bad. She's got a strong motive. And no alibi. But of course, she says she didn't do it."

"She offer any other suspects?"

"She thinks Ms. Lux is the killer."

"Interesting," says Marty. "And what did Ms. Lux say when you asked her about that."

"Asked her about what?"

Marty frowns. "About the chef accusing her of killing the assistant."

"Oh, yes, well, you see … " I trail off, suddenly realizing my mistake.

"Don't tell me," says Marty. "You didn't ask Ms. Lux about the chef's assertion that Ms. Lux is the killer, did you?"

Biting my lip, I say nothing.

After a few moments of silence, Marty says, "Sophia? Did you forget to ask Ms. Lux about the chef's assertion that she's the killer?"

"You told me not to tell you."

Groaning, Marty asks, "What did I do in another life to deserve an employee like you?"

"Yes, I accidentally forgot to ask Ms. Lux about that," I admit. "But, all is not lost ..."

Marty scoffs. "You want to bet?"

"Not really," I say, shaking my head. "I'm not good at gambling. When I used to go to the goat races with my dad, I never picked the winning goat."

Marty glares at me. "Is this one of those moments when you're being obtuse on purpose?"

"I don't think so ..."

Throwing up his hands, Marty says, "Okay, I'm curious. Why is all not lost?"

"Well, I'm glad you asked," I say, smiling. "After I questioned Ms. Lux about her assistant, I questioned her driver, Esteban, who gave me way more information. And an intriguing theory."

"Which is?"

"The assistant was killed protecting the dog," I say. "And maybe he's right. Maybe the dognapper killed the assistant because she wouldn't let them take the Corgi. If you find the dognapper then you find the killer."

"So do it ..." says Marty.

"Do what?"

"Find the dognapper," says Marty. "And in doing so, find the killer."

"Speaking of the dognapper," I start.

"You have any ideas about who might have taken the dog?" asks Marty.

"None whatsoever," I confess. "But, I think the article that Ms.

Lux wants me to write about James Mortimer's disappearance will garner lots of tips, especially when they see the photo of the Corgi. And speaking of that ..."

"Speaking of what?"

"Well, Ms. Lux's driver, Esteban—who's going to send me a photo of the dog—told me some super interesting things about the dog."

"Super interesting?"

"First off, he's a purebred Corgi. Isn't that so super cool?" I ask.

Marty shrugs. "If you say so ..."

"And he was gifted to Ms. Lux by none other than the King of England!"

"You don't say ..."

"Can you believe that?" My hand brushes something cold and hard. Something that seems to be moving. Something ...

I grab the unidentified object and lift it from my purse.

Grasped in my fingers, the little turtle stares at me.

Screaming, I jump up and toss the turtle away from me. "Ohmigoodness!"

It lands in Marty's lap.

Cursing, he grabs it, jumps up, and screams as he tosses it back toward me. "What is that thing?"

"It's a turtle," I say as I catch it, and throw the turtle back at Marty.

"What are you doing with a turtle?" Marty catches the turtle.

"It was in my purse," I say, recalling the last turtle that Esteban was unable to locate.

"Why was a turtle in your purse?" asks Marty, holding the turtle eye level, examining it.

"Well, I think—"

"Hey, what's going on?" asks Clark, stepping into Marty's office. "I could hear you guys—"

"Here, get rid of this thing!" shouts Marty, throwing the turtle at Clark.

Clark shouts in shock, or possibly surprise, maybe both, then catches the turtle, fumbling the little creature. "What is this?"

"It's a turtle," I say. "It was in my purse."

"Why was it in your purse?" asks Clark, as he tosses the turtle back to me.

"It accidentally crawled into my purse when I was at Lucretia Lux's beach house," I say, catching the turtle and tossing it back to Marty.

"Sophia, will you stop throwing this turtle at me!" yells Marty. "I don't want this thing."

"I don't want it, either," I say, prepared to duck if Marty lobs the turtle in my direction again.

"Why were you at Lucretia Lux's beach house?" asks Clark, catching the turtle with one hand when Marty tosses it at him.

"I went there to interview her for a follow-up story about the dog park murder," I explain, bobbing and weaving as Clark raises his hand, prepared to throw the turtle back to me. "Some turtles from the lake behind her house got onto the terrace and her driver was supposed to round them up and take them back to the lake but he only found two of the turtles and—"

Clark throws the turtle at me.

I squeal and duck, but I can't get out of the way in time.

The turtle smacks me in the face.

"Sophie!" cries Clark, rushing toward me. "I'm sorry!"

"It's okay," I say, looking up into Clark's dreamy eyes, even though it's sort of not okay. "I know you didn't mean for me to get a face full of turtle."

A smile playing at the corner of Clark's mouth, he says, "I've got antibacterial wipes at my desk."

"Clark, did you forget that antibiotics put me in a coma?" I ask, as Clark and I head out of Marty's office.

"Oh, yeah, that's right," Clark says. "We better stick with soap and water."

"Wait!" shouts Marty. "Where are you going?"

I turn and then press a hand over my mouth, stifling a laugh.

Marty is standing on his desk, scanning the floor.

Unable to hold his laughter, Clark sniggles.

"This is not funny!" shouts Marty.

"Actually, it kind of is," I tell him.

"Where is the turtle?" demands Marty. "Do you see him?"

Clark and I look around, but the turtle is nowhere to be found.

"Maybe it crawled away," I suggest, grabbing my oversized bag and swinging it onto my shoulder.

"Or maybe it's hiding," says Clark.

"Yeah, that's what I'm afraid of," says Marty, carefully climbing down from his desk.

Shocked, I ask, "You're afraid of turtles?"

"No, I am not afraid of turtles. I just don't want a wayward turtle roaming around my office," says Marty, picking up the receiver of his desk phone and jabbing his index fingers against several buttons. "Candace ... I need you. There's a turtle on the loose in my office and I need you to find it!"

Chapter 10

"So, what's the tea on my owner, sis?" asks Callie.

Glancing at the Calico, who lounges in the passenger seat of my JEEP, I sigh.

A long, eventful day is coming to an end.

I should be headed home to enjoy the sunset as I lounge on my patio while sipping a mug of steaming hot passionfruit tea with mango-glazed donut holes. And while enjoying the tea as I marvel at the pink and lavender sky, I should bask in the warm, balmy glow of praise Marty heaped upon me during the quick, impromptu status meeting regarding my dog park murder articles. And while I'm reflecting on Marty's praise, I'll remind myself that, technically, it wasn't exactly praise. Neither was it criticism or disapproval. Actually, it was more like a bitter, grudging, reluctant admission that my dog park murder stories are performing better than he expected, which I decided was praise—that is, coming from Marty.

Anyhoo, I should be doing anything other than what I'm doing at the moment, which is driving to the little village of Pebble Republic. It's a lively enclave on the far northern tip of St. Mateo, where working-class islanders live in brightly colored row houses along the outskirts of the jungle.

Callie and I are going to take her back to her real human.

His name is Sebastian Smith, and he lives at 12 Papaya Park Circle in Pebble Republic.

Obviously, I'm not excited about this trip, but I promised Callie I would return her to her rightful owner, and I'm going to stay true to my word. Truthfully, I'm a bit devastated about having to give Callie up, but I will.

"What do you know about this guy?" asks the cat.

"Actually, not much," I admit. "Just his name, really …"

"Shouldn't you know more than just his name?" demands the cat. "Or do you plan to just hand me over to some stranger?"

"Well, no, but …" I trail off. Honestly, I wanted to find out more about Callie's real owner. Specifically, I wanted to know how Callie got lost. And once the owner realized Callie was gone, what did he do? Has the real owner been looking for her? Did he contact the island animal shelters? Did he put up flyers? Did he employ various social media sites to aid in his search? And, most importantly, did he look for Callie after he realized she was missing?

"I won't be handing you over to a stranger," I insist, though I wish I could be sure that I'm returning Callie to a loving, compassionate owner. I want to know that she'll be in a safe and comfortable environment, one where she'll get to exercise her independence and won't be confined to a pet carrier or put on a leash or cat harness. "You'll be going back to your real human."

Saying nothing, the cat grooms herself.

I wish I knew what she was thinking. I think she's upset with me, and I don't blame her. I should have found out more about her real human. But, the truth is, I didn't really want to … because I didn't really want to find Callie's real owner. I don't want to give her back. And yet, I promised I would, so …

Fifteen minutes later, after following the GPS instructions, I pull up alongside the curb in front of a house the color of passionfruit with yellow trim. 12 Papaya Park Circle.

"Are you sure this is the right address, sis?" asks Callie, standing on her hind legs with her front paws pressed against the window.

"This is where the GPS told us to go," I say.

"Where are the papaya trees?" asks Callie, looking back at me. "Where is the park? Why isn't the street circular?"

"You know, I'm not sure," I say, agreeing with Callie's assessment. There are no papaya trees, there's no park nearby and the street is not a circle. My heart pounds. Part of me wants to turn around and speed home, but another part knows I have to keep my promise to Callie.

Settling back into the passenger seat, Callie licks her front paw.

Swallowing my reservations, I say, "Well ... shall we go and meet your owner?"

The cat looks at me. "I guess so ..."

The slight reluctance in the cat's tone makes me pause. I don't want to read too much into things, but I wonder if Callie is dreading this meeting with her real owner as much as I am. Then again, Callie can be indifferent sometimes. I might be mistaking nonchalance for worry.

After a few minutes of hesitation, during which time I try to convince myself that I am doing the right thing, I get out of the JEEP, with much grudging reluctance. Callie follows me and together we walk to the front door. As I knock on the weathered wood, I'm hoping Sebastian Smith isn't home. Or, if he is home, then maybe he's forgotten about Callie. Or, if he is home and he does remember Callie, then maybe, after he finds out about my special bond with the feisty feline, he'll come to the conclusion that she belongs with me, and he'll relinquish his rights as her human, and—

The door opens.

My heart slams as I stare at the little old man staring at me through glasses as thick as cut crystal.

"Can I help you?" asks the old man.

"Girl, that can't be my real owner," says the cat. "He looks nothing like a cat dad."

"You don't think so?" I mumble to the Calico, focusing on the cinnamon-colored freckles dusted across his long, bulbous nose.

"Beg your pardon?" asks the elderly man.

"He's definitely a dog person," says Callie.

"Um, yes, well, actually …" I clear my throat and try to give him a smile. "Good evening, I don't mean to disturb you, but are you Sebastian Smith?"

"Sebastian Smith?" The little old man pulls his jacket tight and shivers, even though it's a typical balmy island evening. "No, that's not me."

"Did you ask him if he's my owner?" demands Callie.

"Not yet," I whisper down to the cat, then ask the man, "Is Sebastian Smith home, by any chance?"

"Is he home?" The old man frowns. "I have no idea whether Sebastian Smith is home, or not. He might be, but I don't know."

"What are you waiting for, sis?" asks Callie. "Ask him so he can tell you that he's not my owner and we can make like a tree and leave!"

Ignoring Callie, I ask the man, "Well, could you check?"

The old man blinks behind the glasses, which are smudged. "Check what?"

"Check and see if Sebastian is home?" I ask.

"So, the old man is not Sebastian?" asks Callie. "Why am I not surprised? Girl, I told you he wasn't my owner."

"How would I do that?" The old man appears puzzled. "I don't know where Sebastian Smith lives. I don't even know Sebastian Smith."

"Wait. Sebastian Smith doesn't live here?"

"So, this is not my real owner's house?" the cat demands to know. "Girl, I knew we were at the wrong address. You must have followed the wrong directions."

"No, he does not. Nobody lives here but me and I'm not Sebastian Smith," says the old man. "My name is Elmer Fletcher."

"Elmer Fletcher?" Confused, I ask, "Is this 12 Papaya Park Circle?"

"Who is Elmer Fletcher?" demands Callie.

"It most certainly is 12 Papaya Park Circle and has been for the past fifty years since my father built it with his bare hands," says Mr. Fletcher.

Glancing at the houses to the right and left of Mr. Fletcher's house, I ask, "Is it possible that Sebastian Smith is one of your neighbors, or—"

"No, Sebastian Smith is not my neighbor," says Mr. Fletcher. "I know all my neighbors. None of them is named Smith. I think maybe you got the wrong street. Maybe the wrong neighborhood."

"Yeah, maybe so," I agree. "Sorry to bother you."

Ten minutes later, as I drive home, Callie chatters on and on about how she knew the old guy wasn't her owner and that I had driven to the wrong address.

"Girl, didn't I tell you that cats know things?"

"Yeah, that's what you're always telling me."

"And that's what you need to remember, sis," informs Callie as she curls into a ball on the passenger seat. Soon, she's asleep, and I'm feeling conflicted. On the one hand, part of me is thrilled that Elmer Fletcher wasn't Sebastian Smith. But another part of me realizes that I still need to find Callie's owner. I must have the wrong information about Sebastian Smith. That means I need to do a bit of digging to get the right address. I'm not looking forward to that, but I made Callie a promise.

Braking at a red traffic light, I glance at the Calico.

No matter what, no matter how heartbreaking it will be to return her to her rightful owner, I have to keep my word.

Chapter 11

"Day drinking, sis?"

The sassy sarcasm brightens my spirits and lifts my mood, even though I didn't feel dispirited or moody. As a matter of fact, I was enjoying my second steaming cup of lemon lavender tea with coconut donut holes while I relaxed on the patio, happy to spend a lazy Sunday morning doing nothing.

"Callie!" I call out, swinging my legs off the lounge and placing my feet on the ground. The feline makes a graceful leap from the balcony railing to the space on the lounge I made for her.

"How've you been, girl?"

"Pretty good."

"Where have you been?"

Two days ago, I thought I'd be returning Callie to her owner. But I got the wrong house. Sebastian Smith doesn't live at 12 Papaya Park Circle. So I didn't have to give Callie up. Although, honestly, Callie doesn't belong to me, so I technically don't have the right to return her to her real human. But, I'm supposed to find her owner, which I plan to do.

Still, until I find her owner's right address, I want to spend as much time with the cat as possible. As much time as she'll allow me to be with her.

"You know me, sis," says the cat, licking her fur. "I've been out and about."

Resisting the urge to scratch behind Callie's ear, I say, "Being independent."

"And finding out things," says the cat.

"What things?" I ask, taking a sip of tea. "Did you find out what happened to Lucretia Lux's missing Corgi?"

"Not yet, but let me ask you something," says Callie, staring at me. "Did you smuggle a turtle from Lucretia Lux's beach house back to the *Palmchat Gazette* office two days ago?"

"Smuggle a turtle? No! Wait. Are you talking about the turtle who crawled into my bag without telling me and that I only discovered when I was in Marty's office and I reached in my bag to get my phone and—"

"Right, girl," says Callie, bobbing her head. "That turtle."

"Wait. What do you know about that turtle?" I ask. "The last time I saw the turtle was in Marty's office before he disappeared under the desk or went into hiding, or—"

"The turtle ended up in the ladies' room."

"The ladies' room?"

"Apparently, your dingbat coworker Candace found the turtle in your manager's office," says the feline. "Then she took him to the ladies' room, gave him a bath in one of the sinks, and then he bit your dingbat coworker so she left him in the ladies' room."

"What? How did I not know about this?" I ask, and then recall that Candace has been out for the last two days, and Marty grumbled something about a finger injury when I asked him where she was.

"Anyway," says Callie, licking her left foot. "Sammy Alastair—you remember him, right?"

"The rat who lives in the ladies' room and eats roaches," I say, shuddering in disgust. "How could I forget?"

"Girl, don't be sarcastic. Especially not at eight in the morning. It's not a good look," admonishes the cat.

"Sorry ..." I mumble and then sip more tea.

"Besides, I told you. Sammy's a good egg," says Callie. "After all, rats gonna rat, right? Case in point: Sammy told me the turtle has information about the dog park murder story you're working on."

Intrigued, I ask, "What kind of information?"

"That's what we have to find out," says the cat. "Sammy and the turtle are waiting for us in the ladies' room at the *Palmchat Gazette*."

"What? Wait!" Confused, I jump up. "They are? Now? In the ladies' room?"

"Yes, they are. Now. In the ladies' room," confirms the cat. "So, come on, sis, let's go!"

Chapter 12

"Before the turtle spills any tea," announces Callie, "he wants an official apology from you."

Confused, I ask, "An apology from me? What? Why?"

Instead of the ladies' restroom, Callie and I decided to meet Sammy Alastair, and the turtle, whose name is Tyrone, in one of the empty guest cubicles in the newsroom. At the moment, I'm sitting on the desk with my feet in the chair. Callie is lounging on the desk next to me. Sammy is scurrying across the floor. And the turtle is hanging out near the waste basket.

"Something about you and your coworkers using him to play Hot Potato," says Callie.

"Oh. Yes, well, um, that ..." I trail off, recalling how Marty, Clark, and I tossed the turtle back and forth without regard for his safety or mental well-being. "Please tell the turtle that I am sincerely sorry and that I regret my actions but explain that I was shocked and nervous to find him in my purse and I panicked."

Callie relays my message.

The turtle responds with a few clucks, a few high-pitched whines, and a hiss.

"What did he say?" I ask, worried that the turtle will refuse my apology and decline to spill the tea.

"He says that if it happens again," begins Callie, "he'll send Gamera to destroy you."

"Gamera?" I'm confused. "Wait. Does he mean the fictional Japanese monster from the Godzilla movies?"

Callie seeks additional clarity from the turtle.

"Yeah, that Gamera," says the feline.

"What? Wait. Ask him if he knows that Gamera isn't real?"

Callie relays my question.

The turtle hisses and whines.

The cat looks at me. "Girl, Gamera is real to Tyrone, so if I were you, sis, I wouldn't use him to play Hot Potato again."

"Fine, fine," I agree. "Can he spill the tea now?"

As Callie starts to speak, the rat begins to squeak.

"Okay, Sammy … I'll tell her. I'll tell her," says Callie.

"You'll tell who what?"

Staring at me, Callie says, "Sammy wants your assurance that the janitor will stop putting out mouse traps to try to kill him."

The rat lets forth another bout of squeaking.

Callie bobs her head, then says to me, "Sammy says that the janitor should thank him because Sammy is getting rid of the roaches which means the newspaper is paying the janitor for a job he's not even doing, which is unethical, and—"

"Okay, okay," I say, eager to get the turtle's tea, which I'm hoping is piping hot. "Tell Sammy I'll talk to the janitor."

After Callie gives the rat my assurance, the turtle starts clucking and whining.

When he pipes down, Callie looks at me. "So according to the turtle, who spends a lot of time on Lucretia Lux's terrace, even though Ms. Lux hates turtles, on the day when the assistant was killed, Ms. Lux and Annie Stone had a huge argument out on the terrace."

The turtle clucks.

Callie says, "Annie Stone wanted to be in the new movie that Lucretia Lux is planning to produce, but Lucretia Lux said no way, not today, and not tomorrow, either."

"Interesting," I say. "And then what happened?"

Callie asks the turtle to continue.

The turtle whines for what seems like a full minute.

Staring at me, Callie says, "Girl, you are not going to believe this! Apparently, Annie Stone had a video of Ms. Lux kicking her dog."

"I do believe it," I tell Callie. "I know about the video footage."

"How?"

"Bonnie Lambeaux told me."

Callie says, "Well, did you know that Annie Stone threatened to sell the video to the media and release it all over the internet if Ms. Lux didn't allow her to co-star in the movie?"

"Are you kidding?"

The turtle clucks a few more times.

Staring at me, Callie says, "The turtle says that Ms. Lux grabbed Annie and slapped her."

Shocked, I echo, "Ms. Lux slapped Annie?"

Callie says, "She didn't just slap her, girl. Ms. Lux also told Annie that if she released the video, she would kill her … "

Chapter 13

Wrapping my hands around my mug, I take a sip of the divine coconut and lime tea.

It's three in the afternoon and I'm thinking about the information the turtle spilled, which makes me more inclined to believe that Ms. Lux could have killed her assistant. By my estimation—not that I'm any good at estimating, mind you—Ms. Lux had more to lose than Chef Bonnie.

Sure, Annie was blackmailing Bonnie, which gives Bonnie a motive. However, a video of Lucretia Lux kicking her dog—who is just about as famous and beloved as she is—would ruin her career. The public outcry would be deafening. People would hate her. If Annie was going to sell the tape to the media, Ms. Lux probably felt she had to stop her.

But was killing Annie the only way to stop the blackmail?

Technically, Ms. Lux could have stopped the blackmail if she'd given Annie Stone a role in the new movie she was producing, but Ms. Lux didn't want to do that.

I take another sip of tea and glance at my computer.

Earlier this morning, while I worked on fact-checking some

articles I'd written, I kept an eye out on the paper's social media feeds. I'm happy to report that the James Mortimer dognapping story is trending like crazy. Even better, my article has been picked up and reported on by several leading news publications around the globe. Of course, the social media accounts of Ms. Lux and James Mortimer have been flooded with comments, likes, and shares.

Everyone seems heartbroken about James Mortimer's disappearance. Several websites and social media accounts have been created with the sole purpose of gathering information to find the Corgi.

Nevertheless, Marty still made time to remind me that, despite the good news, he expects me to stay on top of my assignments and follow-up stories. As he put it, "You're still on probation, Sophia. One trending story is not enough to save your job. Drop the ball on any of your other articles and you're out of here."

Speaking of my story assignments, I shift my focus back to the murder of Annie Stone.

So far, I would say the suspects are Lucretia Lux, Bonnie Lambeaux, and … the dognapper. Not that I'm sure there even is a dognapper. Sure, Ms. Lux thinks James Mortimer was taken, and her driver, Esteban, agrees, but is that true? Nevertheless, I have to admit, the dognapping murderer theory is intriguing.

With that in mind, I pick up my desk phone and call the St. Mateo police department. When the desk sergeant picks up, I ask to be connected to Officer Noah Cuetee.

"Hey, Sophie, what's going on?"

"Do you have a minute?"

"I have about ten," he says. "And then I have to head out."

"Okay, I'll try to get all of this out in ten minutes, or less," I promise. "It's about the dog park murder. I got some information from an anonymous source."

"What's the info?"

"I think Detective François might need to take a look at Lucretia Lux as a suspect in the murder of Annie Stone," I say, and then go on to spill the tea that the turtle gave me about Ms. Lux slapping Annie Stone and threatening to kill the assistant.

"Interesting," says Officer Cuetee.

"Does Detective François suspect Ms. Lux?"

Officer Cuetee sighs. "I'm not sure. You know how François likes to keep his thoughts to himself. But I'll mention the threat. Maybe he'll question Ms. Lux again."

"What did Ms. Lux say when Detective François questioned her?"

"She didn't actually talk to him," says Officer Cuetee. "Ms. Lux provided a statement through her attorney. François wasn't very happy about that. But the statement was a generic denial of any knowledge of or involvement in the murder of Annie Stone."

"Not surprising," I say.

"Hey, Sophie, I've got to get going," says Officer Cuetee. "But how about we get together for tea soon?"

Smiling to myself, I say, "Absolutely!"

Chapter 14

"Girl, what are you doing?"

Breaking out of the spin I was just doing, I skitter to a stop and face the feline, who perches on the balcony railing of my patio. Normally, my evenings are spent watching the St. Mateo sunset with a mug of tea—preferably peppermint, but spearmint works great also —but when I arrived home, I found myself in a Broadway musical mood, for some reason.

Although, I suspect the reason is because while I was buying tea at lunch, the tea shop was playing the soundtrack to The Sound of Music.

Anyway, after doing some online research to learn how to properly execute ballet moves, I retreated to the patio to practice pirouetting, which is what I tell the cat.

Callie looks at me. "And why are you practicing doing pirouettes? You planning on joining the Palmchat Gazette Ballet Company?"

"Not exactly," I say, pirouetting over to the lounge where I plop down. "So, what's up? Did you drop by to say "hi"? Or maybe hang out? We can watch old episodes of Tom and Jerry."

Licking her fur, the cat says, "Tom and Jerry? Girl, whatever. I'm here to help you keep your job so your boss won't ship you out."

"You have information about the dog park murder? The missing Corgi?"

"I found out that the assistant had a diary," says Callie. "There's a mouse in the beach house. He's going to tell us where the diary is hidden."

"He is?" I ask. "Wait. Why do we need this diary?"

"Apparently, the assistant wrote all her secrets in the diary," says the cat. "The mouse was present when the assistant journaled. Sometimes, as she wrote, she said out loud what she was writing. The mouse heard something about someone wanting to kill the assistant."

"Are you serious?"

"I'm thinking maybe the assistant knew her killer," theorizes the cat.

"That's possible," I say.

Bobbing her head, Callie says, "So we need to go to the beach house and get that diary."

"How do we do that?"

"Girl, I just told you. The mouse is going to show us where the assistant hid the diary," says the feisty feline. "Were you listening?"

"Yes, I was listening," I jump up and pace in front of the lounge. "But, I can't just show up at Ms. Lux's beach house and say, Hi, Ms. Lux, I'm here to search your beach house for a diary that belonged to your assistant which might contain the name of her killer, which might be you, or maybe your personal chef. I'm not sure."

"Why can't you say that?" asks the cat. "I swear, you humans never say what you really mean to each other. That's why you never get along with each other."

Exhaling, I say, "You may be right about that. Nevertheless, Ms.

Lux is not going to just invite me into her house so I can go snooping around—"

"You won't have to snoop," says Callie. "I swear, you really are deaf in one ear and can't hear out of the other one. I just said the mouse will show us where the diary is."

"Okay. Fine." I blow out a frustrated breath. "Still, if I show up at the beach house, I'll need a good excuse for why I'm there."

"Girl, I'm sure you'll think of something," says the feline as she jumps from the balcony railing to the ground. "You went to college, right?"

"Yes, I went to college."

"Then act like it," instructs the cat. "Now, let's go."

"Wait. What? We have to go now?"

The cat gives me a look. "Girl, did I stutter?"

Resigned, I sigh. "Okay. Let me get my purse and car keys."

Chapter 15

"I'm sorry, but Ms. Lux isn't home," says Esteban, Ms. Lux's driver. Standing behind the threshold of the twelve-foot mahogany wood door, he stares at me with curiosity and suspicion.

"Oh, no worries," I assure him. "Actually, I wanted to talk to you."

"Talk to me?" Esteban frowns. "About what?"

"Well …" I start, clearing my throat.

As Callie and I drove from my apartment to Ms. Lux's beach house, we devised a reason for my visit which seemed like a good idea as I steered the JEEP along the winding roads. With the sky-streaked pink and orange, and my favorite CoCo song as background music, I felt bold and empowered. Like a gutsy, no-holds-barred investigative reporter.

Now that I'm standing in front of Esteban, who looks distracted and slightly annoyed to see me, I'm not so sure I can—

"Girl, what are you waiting on?" demands Callie, who's sitting at my feet, behind my left heel. "We do not have all night. We have to get the assistant's diary and find out if she wrote down the name of her killer."

Lowering my head slightly, glancing down at the cat, I whisper, "Yes, I know that ..."

"Yes, you know what?"

Shocked that he heard me, I clear my throat and take a step closer to him. "I recently received information suggesting that Ms. Lux may have had something to do with the death of Annie Stone. So, I wanted to—"

"I don't know what information you're talking about," interrupts Esteban. "But, whoever told you that ..."

"That ...?" I prompt.

Esteban sniffs as his eyes flutter. "Whoever told you that ... Ms. Lux had ..."

"Had ...?"

Expelling a coughing gasp, Esteban sniffs again as his eyes squeeze shut.

"Esteban?" I ask, worried.

"Ah ... ahh ... ahhh ... " The driver's head whips back as his mouth opens.

"Girl, what is wrong with him?" asks Callie.

"I'm not sure," I whisper.

"I don't know about you, sis," says the cat. "But I'm about to get out of the way."

"Esteban? Are you—"

The driver expels a violent sneeze. "*Ah-CHOO!!*"

"Omigoodness!" Squealing, I jump back as Esteban stumbles forward, propelled by the force of his sneeze.

"*Ahhh ... CHOO!!!*" Esteban sneezes again, stumbling back, eyes closed, one hand pressed against his nose.

"Oh, Esteban!" I cry, side-stepping away from him.

"Do ... you ... *ah-choo!* ... have a ... *ah-choo!* ... cat?" demands Esteban, sounding as though his nose is stuffed. "*Ahhh ... CHOO!*"

"Do I have a cat? No, no I don't have a cat," I say.

"Let him know, sis," advises Callie.

"Yes ... you ... *ah-choo*!" With one eye open, Esteban points toward a large metal planter. "You do have a cat!"

I follow his finger and glance down at Callie, who's licking her fur.

"Oh. No. That's not my cat," I tell him. "Well, she's a cat I know. But she's not my cat."

"Get that ... *ah-choo* ... cat ... *ah-choo*!" Esteban's body arcs and quakes with each violent sneeze he expels.

"Omigoodness!" I say. "You're allergic to cats!"

"You have to ... ah-choo ... get the cat ... ah-choo!"

Trying to follow his words, and stay away from his propulsive sneezes, I take a step back. "I have to what?"

Shaking his head, Esteban turns and flees into the house.

"Girl, what was his problem?" asks Callie.

"He's allergic to you," I tell her.

"Well, he needs to take allergy medicine," advises the cat as she walks pass me, over the threshold, and into the foyer.

"Wait. Callie. What are you doing?" I ask, hesitant to follow the fearless feline. "Where are you going?"

Callie looks back at me. "Come on, sis. We have to talk to the mouse."

"What? No! Callie, we can't ..." I trail off as my protests fall on deaf ears. Frozen in place, I groan. Callie is known for her willingness to brazenly go wherever she wants ... even if it's into someone else's house uninvited. I don't know how many times I've tried to tell her that we can't just go into a person's home without their permission. Nevertheless, the cat doesn't care.

Exhaling, I take a few tentative steps forward until I'm over the threshold and standing in the foyer. I glance around the expansive entryway, which is as wide as the width of my bedroom, and decorated in muted tones of beige, sand, and tan.

"Callie …?" I whisper, walking forward as I glance back, wondering if I should close the door, or—

"Girl, what took you so long?" demands the cat.

"I don't think we should be in Ms. Lux's house without her knowing—"

"Sis, whatever," says the feline. "We need to talk to the mouse and since the driver is off somewhere having a sneezing fit, we need to take advantage of his allergy."

"Oh, Callie, that's not nice," I tell her. "Allergies are horrible."

"Girl, murder is horrible, too," the cat tells me. "Now, do you want to find out who killed the assistant, or do you want your boss to think that you're a horrible reporter and fire you? Just let me know. Because if you don't want to talk to the mouse, we can leave. I've got stuff I need to do—"

"Okay, okay …" I sigh. "Let's just talk to the mouse and get the assistant's diary and get out of here before we get thrown out."

"The mouse told me to meet him in the kitchen," says Callie.

"Where is the kitchen?"

"Girl, how should I know?" Callie looks up at me. "Haven't you been here before?"

"Yes, but Ms. Lux didn't give me a grand tour," I say, walking from the foyer into the ginormous living area.

"Well, aren't kitchens usually in the same place in most houses?"

"This is not most houses," I say, marveling at the clusters of sitting areas sectioned in each corner of the living room. The arrangement of U-shaped couches, cane chairs, and wooden coffee tables reminds me of the grand lobby of the Hibiscus Hotel. "This is a giant mansion. The kitchen could literally be anywhere. It could take us days to find it."

The cat walks forward, then stops and turns back to me. "You smell that?"

I sniff the air. "Smell what?"

"Bread. Bananas. Mango. Stale coffee," says Callie. "The kitchen. It's this way. Come on …"

Chapter 16

"So … where is the mouse?" I ask, walking toward the island.

Turns out, Callie was right about the location of the kitchen.

I followed the cat, and her keen sense of smell, down several long wide hallways until we headed through an arched entryway into a large, bright, cheery French country blue and yellow kitchen.

"He's around here somewhere," says Callie. "Let me take a look."

As the cat trots over toward the corner near the refrigerator, I wring my hands and lament that I don't have pearls to clutch. I'm super nervous, worried we'll be caught by Esteban, or some other staff member, and get kicked out before we can get the information about the assistant's diary.

"Hey, sis … over here …"

Following the sound of Callie's voice, I turn.

Across the kitchen, beneath one of the chairs under the large round table, sits Callie, licking her fur. Next to the cat is a little ball of gray fur no bigger than my hand. As I walk closer, the little ball of fur scurries back and forth, scampering around Callie, revealing itself to be a cute little mouse with a pink nose and twitching whiskers.

"This is Klaus," introduces Callie. "Klaus, this is Sophie, my human."

"Hi, Klaus!" I say, giving him a little wave.

The tiny rodent lets forth several high-pitched squeaks.

Callie says, "Stop tripping, Klaus. Sophie's a good egg."

"Yes, please tell him I'm a very good egg," I say, worried. Will Klaus refuse to talk to me if he doesn't think I'm a good egg, of superior quality, from one of the top-producing hens at one of the island's best poultry farms?

Callie says to Klaus, "She's very nice. A little scatter-brained, at times."

"Scatter-brained?" I frown at the cat.

"Somewhat absentminded on occasion," the cat tells the mouse.

"Absentminded?" I dispute.

"But she's pretty smart, too, as far as humans go, and you know humans can't go very far," says Callie to Klaus, who squeals a response that, somehow, sounds suspiciously like laughter.

"Thought you were supposed to be telling Klaus that I'm a good egg," I say.

"Relax, sis," says Callie as Klaus emits a few more squeaks. "No, Klaus, you can trust her. She wouldn't hurt a flea!"

"Make sure he knows that I'm very trustworthy," I say, "And I don't even have fleas so there's no way I could harm them."

Callie gives me a look, and a hiss, then looks down at the mouse. "I understand that you've trusted humans before only to find out that they do, in fact, hurt fleas, but Sophie is not one of those humans."

Klaus scurries around the table legs, then stops in front of Callie and starts squeaking again.

Callie glances up at me. "Klaus will take us to the assistant's room, where we'll find the diary."

"Great!" I say, clapping my hands.

"But we're going to have to do him a favor first," says the cat.
"What kind of favor?" I ask.
The cat says, "Get him some cheese from the refrigerator."

Chapter 17

Ten minutes later, Callie and I, along with Klaus—slightly sluggish from the three cubes of muenster he gobbled down before the three of us left the kitchen—arrive at the assistant's bedroom.

Honestly, I can't believe we got here.

We took so many twists and turns down so many hallways. I kept wishing we had the blueprints for the house. Or, maybe a GPS to give directions. But, the mouse knew the way. Now I'm standing in the middle of a fairly large room, sparsely furnished, and decorated in muted tones. Nothing flashy or fancy. A basic bedroom for a staff member, someone on the payroll who Ms. Lux didn't have to impress with exquisite pieces and vibrant colors.

Wobbling across the sisal natural fiber rug, Klaus starts to squeak.

Callie says, "Klaus says he feels bad about the assistant passing away."

Stopping near the leg of a small desk in the corner, beneath a small window, Klaus continues to chitter.

"The assistant was always nice to him, he says," Callie tells me as she leaps up onto the twin bed. "She gave him lots of cheese. Not just muenster, but gruyere, brie, and sometimes ricotta."

"Well, that was nice of her," I say, glancing over my shoulder. I want to respect Klaus' need to reminisce, but I wish he'd show us where the diary is so Callie and I can scram.

As we made our way from the kitchen to the servants' wing, I couldn't help being nervous, worried that Esteban, or worse, Ms. Lux, would catch me and demand to know, forthwith, what on earth I was doing. And what could I say? Looking for a diary which I hope will contain the name of Annie Stone's killer, which might very well be you.

Klaus squeaks and squeals.

Licking her fur, Callie says, "Listen, Klaus, we get it, okay? Annie was kind to you. Gave you water and didn't set traps to catch you. Great. Where is her diary? Sophie and I don't have time for your eulogizing."

"Callie!" I scold, even though I was pretty much thinking the same thing.

Klaus squeals and squeaks.

Callie glances at me. "The diary is beneath the desk chair."

"Beneath the desk chair?" I frown, confused as I stare at the plain, wooden straight-backed chair pushed beneath the small desk. The floor beneath the desk is clear. "There's nothing beneath the chair."

"Under the seat, sis," says Callie.

"Under the seat …" I mumble to myself as I walk to the chair.

Klaus chitters.

Callie says, "Get on your hands and knees and look upside down under the chair."

"Oh, I get it …" I say, then follow the cat's instructions.

Poking my head between the legs and under the seat, I turn my head until I can view the frame supporting the seat. On the underside of the seat, between the corner blocks, is a pale pink 5 x 7 journal held in place by a wide swath of gray electrical tape.

"Do you see it?" asks the cat.

"It's taped to the chair," I say, maneuvering onto my back and positioning my head beneath the chair.

"Wonder why she did that?" asks Callie.

"Obviously she didn't want anyone to find it," I say.

"Which means it must contain the killer's identity," says the cat.

"Hopefully," I say, giving the tape a few more yanks until I rip it away and free the journal. "Got it!"

"You got what …?"

I freeze, recognizing the voice, even though it sounds stuffy.

It's Esteban …

Chapter 18

"Hello ..." says Esteban.

Cringing and concerned by the harsh accusation in his tone, I lift my head and—

Bang it against the frame beneath the seat. "Owwww!!!"

Footsteps tread closer. "What are you doing ... ah-CHOO! Ah-CHOO!"

Sliding from beneath the chair, I glance up.

Esteban's head arcs back as his body arches into a boomerang shape and he lets forth another string of sneezes. Taking advantage of his allergic predicament, I roll over onto my side, sit up, and quickly shove the assistant's journal into the large bag on my shoulder.

"Think it's time for me to scram," says Callie, trotting quickly toward the door as Esteban sneezes again, a volcanic explosion that sends him whirling like a dervish.

"You can't leave me," I tell the cat as I scramble to my feet.

"Girl, you got this," says Callie as she exits, stage left, with Klaus scurrying at her heels.

Clearing my throat, I smooth my skirt and attempt a smile as

Esteban grabs a tissue from the box on the night table next to the bed.

"I don't see a cat anywhere," I say, pretending to look around.

Esteban blows his nose, reminding me of an out-of-tune trumpet.

"You know, maybe I should just leave now …" I suggest, heading for the door.

Esteban steps in front of me, blocking my path. Sniffing, he says, "Maybe you should tell me what you're doing in here?"

"Well, yes, right, you see, um …" I exhale. "I actually got lost. This is such a big house and—"

"You got lost in Annie's room?"

"Oh. What? Really?" I give a weak laugh. "This was Annie's room. Wow. Gosh. I didn't know …"

"You sure about that?"

"How could I know?"

Esteban's eyes narrow, and he doesn't say anything but I can tell he's suspicious of me.

"Anyway … I was, um …" I swallow. "Well, the cat ran into the house and I ran in after her, and—"

"She ran into Annie's room?"

"The cat ran all over the house," I say. "And, as I said, I was trying to find her and I thought I saw her come into this room and maybe she did because you started to sneeze but she's not in here now and I really need to find her, and—"

"I thought you said she wasn't your cat."

"Yes, right, well, you know …" I attempt another smile. "She's not, but … I should probably go."

"What did you want to ask me?"

I blink, staring at him. "What?"

"I thought you came here to ask me some questions," says the driver, giving me a shrewd look.

"Yes, right, well, um … " I move my oversized bag from my left shoulder to my right. "Recently, I received an anonymous tip from someone who alleged that Ms. Lux killed Annie Stone."

Esteban frowns. "Who told you that?"

"An anonymous source," I say, hoping he won't press the issue, since I can't tell him that my anonymous source is a turtle. Although, even if my anonymous source wasn't a turtle, I still couldn't tell him—

"Why does this … *anonymous source* … think that Ms. Lux killed Annie?"

"Well, because the anonymous source saw Ms. Lux slap Annie and threaten to kill her," I say.

"What evidence does the … anonymous source … have to back up this claim that Ms. Lux slapped Annie and threatened to kill her?"

"What evidence?" I ask, contemplating the question as I ponder the reason for Esteban's emphasis of anonymous source.

"When did they see Ms. Lux slap Annie and threaten to kill her?" demands Esteban.

Struggling to remember the exact details of the turtle's claims, I stutter, "Well, yes, you see, I'm not exactly sure, but—"

"Don't you think you should make sure," says Esteban, scowling. "Before you publish a bunch of unfounded accusations."

"Well, I was trying to make sure the accusations weren't unfounded," I say. "That's why I asked you—"

"You know, you were right," says Esteban.

"About …?"

"Leaving," he says, stepping aside, giving me a clear pathway to the door. "You should go."

"But, was the anonymous source, right?" I ask. "Did Ms. Lux—"

"I think you should go before I call the police," says Esteban, scowling, his tone threatening. "Unless you want to be arrested for trespassing on private property?"

"Yes, right," I say, then clarify, "I mean, no … I don't want to be arrested. Sorry. I'm leaving now …"

Hurrying past Esteban, and his suspicious glare, I exit Annie's room.

Chapter 19

An hour later, back at my apartment, I toss the assistant's diary on the dining room table and head into the kitchen.

I'm anxious to read the journal, but I have a feeling it will contain explosive revelations—that is, I expect Annie Stone will have written about the person who killed her—and I need tea to prepare myself.

Specifically, I'm going to make a mug of lemon and raspberry tea. The lemon will help me manage my excitement and the raspberry will calm my nerves. It's a great combination to drink while discovering the identity of a cold-hearted killer.

If, in fact, the name of the killer is actually written in the journal.

As I grab a mug from an overhead cabinet, I realize I must mentally prepare myself for the fact that Annie Stone might not have written her killer's name in the diary, despite what the mouse claimed. Filling my tea kettle with water, I recall what the mouse claimed.

Apparently, the assistant wrote all her secrets in the diary. The mouse was present when the assistant journaled. Sometimes, as she wrote, she said out loud what she was writing. The mouse heard something about someone wanting to kill the assistant.

I put the tea kettle on the stove and turn the knob to HIGH.

Just because the assistant wrote about someone wanting to kill her doesn't mean that person killed her. After all, the assistant could have been exaggerating. Suppose she was writing about stepping on someone's toe and that person looked at her like they wanted to kill her. Doesn't really mean that person wanted to murder the assistant. The mouse could have gotten things completely out of context.

I drop the tea bag into my mug.

Then again, the assistant might have written about her murderer who might have been Ms. Lux. Perhaps Annie Stone wrote about blackmailing Lucretia Lux. She could have detailed how Ms. Lux grew tired of her demands and threatened to kill her.

The tea kettle whistles.

Startled, I jump. Spurred by the whistling and the steam spiraling from the spout, I grab the kettle and fill my mug with boiling hot water.

However, Annie Stone might have written that Chef Bonnie wanted to kill her. Sure, Bonnie denied it, but the evidence against her seems solid. I put the kettle on a trivet, then pick up my mug and walk to the table. The knife used to kill Annie belonged to Chef Bonnie, who has no alibi for the night of the murder but does have a compelling motive. Annie was blackmailing Chef Bonnie.

Seated at the table, I take a cautious sip of tea.

It's perfect, but it would be better with donut holes drizzled with sweet orange-papaya glaze. Alas, I have no donut holes. But I do have a diary to snoop through.

Sitting the mug on the table, I reach for the diary. A thrill of electric anticipation hums through me. It is not lost on me that I might solve a heinous murder today. Doing so will surely get me booked on one of the morning shows. I can see myself now, wearing a fetching outfit as I explain how, through cunning and heart-pounding stealth, I procured the journal. And then I opened it, and—

I cut the fantasy.

If I'm going to be booked on the morning shows for solving the murder of Annie Stone, I need to open her journal and find out who killed her.

After another quick sip of tea for courage, I let out a breath.

I open the diary and start to read.

Almost immediately, I'm frowning, staring at the words. Only, they don't seem to be words. At least, not any words I know. Possibly not any words that anyone knows.

I tilt my head.

The words seem to be weird symbols. Slashes and dashes and dots and curlicues arranged in odd patterns that don't make any sense. At least, not to me.

My heart, stomach, and spirits sinking, I turn the journal upside down. But that doesn't work. The strange symbols didn't magically turn into words I can read. I flip page after page. Nothing but the crazy symbols. Staring at the pages of indecipherable text, I start to think it must be some secret code.

A code Annie concocted to keep her private thoughts completely private.

Closing the journal, I grab my mug of tea and take a sip. Considering that Annie hid her journal under the seat of her chair, I suppose it also makes sense that she wrote in code. That makes me think that she must have identified her killer in the journal.

I lean back in my chair. Annie hid her journal so no one would find it and wrote in code so in case the diary was found, no one would be able to read it.

Why would she go through that trouble?

Obviously, Annie didn't want Ms. Lux, or Bonnie Lambeaux, to find the diary, or understand the text if it was discovered and read. Naturally, that makes me think that either Ms. Lux or Bonnie Lambeaux killed Annie.

But which one?
And how do I prove it?

Chapter 20

"This is not written in some secret code," declares Clark as he flips through the pages of Annie Stone's diary.

As soon as I arrived at work this morning, instead of checking my social media feeds like I normally do, I buzzed Clark and asked him to meet me in the breakroom. After he got a cup of coffee and I fixed myself a mug of pear and dragon fruit tea, we sat at a table in the far corner where I filled Clark in on my adventures at Lucretia Lux's beach house.

Of course, I didn't divulge anything about Callie or Klaus, but Clark didn't question me when I told him anonymous sources put me on the trail of the assistant's journal.

"Are you sure?" I ask, wondering if Clark needs new glasses.

Nodding, Clark says, "It's shorthand."

Confused, I look at the diary, then at Clark, then back at the diary. "Shorthand?"

"You know, speed writing using symbols," says Clark.

"Yeah, I've heard of it," I say, my mind boggled. "Just didn't realize anyone still wrote in shorthand."

"Reporters used to write in shorthand before recording apps," says Clark, giving me a smirk.

Rolling my eyes, I ask, "And you're sure Annie wrote her journal in shorthand."

"I recognize the symbols," says Clark. "My mom was the church secretary and my dad would dictate letters to her. She wrote them in shorthand before she typed them out."

"Wait. You recognize the symbols?" I stare at Clark. "What do the words say? What did Annie write? Did she identify her killer?"

Closing the journal, Clark slides it across the table toward me. "I said I recognize the symbols. But I don't understand them."

Groaning, I say, "You don't? Are you sure?"

"Shorthand is pretty hard to learn," says Clark. "And I never needed to learn it, so ..."

"Wait. Your mom knows shorthand," I say, once again feeling a spark of hope. "Can you ask her to translate the diary?"

"I would, but ... "

"Oh, no, don't tell me," I say, covering my ears.

Clark chuckles. "Mom and dad are helping to build a church in a remote village in Africa. The cell reception is spotty, at best. But, I'll try to contact her."

"Thanks," I say, even though the spark of hope I had just died.

"Hey, I meant to ask you ..."

"What?" I ask, taking another sip of tea.

"You know that cat you know that's not your cat?"

"Callie?"

"Did you find out who her owner is?"

"Yes. And no." I put my mug on the table.

"Yes and no?"

"I don't know," I admit, recalling my attempt to locate Callie's owner.

"You don't know?"

"I don't think so," I say.

"I don't understand," admits Clark.

"Well …" I say, and then go on to tell Clark about my trip to Pebble Republic, where I thought I'd meet Sebastian Smith, but I had the wrong address.

Clark says, "Maybe whoever chipped the cat put in the wrong address."

"You mean like a clerical error?" I nod. "Maybe."

"Well, there might be a way to find out," says Clark.

"You think I should go back to the vet and find out if he has any additional information about Sebastian Smith?"

"If he did, I don't think he'd be authorized to tell you," Clark says. "I was actually thinking of good old-fashioned detective work."

I frown. "Can you elaborate?"

"Look up the name Sebastian Smith," he says. "Then find out the address associated with the name."

"Sounds simple enough," I conclude.

An hour later, I walk into Clark's cube.

"You're not going to believe this," I say, leaning against a tall metal file cabinet.

"What?"

As it turned out, Clark's simple idea of researching the name Sebastian Smith to discover the correct address wasn't so simple. Because as it turned out, there are fourteen Sebastian Smiths in the Palmchat Islands.

Clark stares at me. "Well …"

"So now what?" I complain. "I can't go to all the islands, knocking on fourteen different doors."

"No, but you can call all fourteen Sebastian Smiths," says Clark. "I'm assuming there were phone numbers associated with the addresses."

"Yes, there were, but …"

"But?"

"Not sure I want to make fourteen phone calls," I admit.

Folding his arms across his chest, Clark says, "Do you want to find out who the cat really belongs to, or not?"

Biting my lip, I hesitate.

If I'm being honest, I don't want to find out the address of Callie's owner. I want to keep the feisty feline for myself, even though she's not my cat. But I promised to find out more about her past, and I'm going to keep my word.

"Listen, I'll help you," offers Clark. "We'll split the list."

Smiling, I say, "That's sweet of you."

Looking a tab embarrassed, Clark shrugs. "It's no problem. I was getting ready to take lunch, anyway. I didn't have any plans, so I don't mind taking an hour to do a good deed."

"Great," I say. "I'll go and get the list, and we'll get started."

Thirty minutes later, I'm ready to throw in the towel. Of the seven people with the name SMITH, SEBASTIAN on my half of the list, one didn't pick up the phone, one hung up the phone in my face, and five had never lost a sassy, sarcastic Calico cat named Callie. At this point, I can only hope that Clark located Callie's human. If not, then—

"Any luck?" asks Clark, behind me.

Swiveling in the chair, I face him. "No luck whatsoever. What about you?"

Clark shakes his head. "None of the Sebastian Smiths I called had lost a cat. Actually, none of them even had a cat."

"Same here," I say.

Chapter 21

A long day of slow news is coming to an end, and I for one am glad about it.

All I want to do is grab my oversized bag and my keys, and head home, where I'll make myself a mug of steaming hot tea and watch the sunset on my porch. If I'm lucky, Callie will show up, and I'll fill her in on my efforts to find her real human.

However, I can't leave because the desk phone is ringing.

Scowling, I stare at the phone. I don't want to answer it, but it might be a tip. A real tip. Not someone calling to tell me to brush your teeth before bed or don't put the cart before the horse or don't count your goats before they eat the grass—things I obviously already know.

Pressing the speaker button, I say, "Sophie Carter, how can I help you?"

"Hey, Sophie, I'm glad you answered," says Officer Cuetee.

"I'm glad I picked up," I say. "I was just getting ready to leave."

"Well, I won't keep you long," he says. "I'm taking a quick break. But, I wanted to give you an update on the dog park murder."

"What's happened?" I ask, grabbing a pen and a yellow legal pad.

"Huge developments," says Officer Cuetee. "Bonnie Lambeaux has officially been cleared as a suspect. She was released from jail this morning."

"Wait. What?" I'm floored. "Bonnie didn't kill Annie Stone?"

"The knife used to kill Annie Stone was not Bonnie's knife," says Officer Cuetee.

"It wasn't?" I ask, jotting notes on the legal pad.

"Not according to the forensic pathologist," says Officer Cuetee. "Annie Stone was murdered with a Swiss Army knife."

"Any idea who the Swiss Army knife belonged to?"

"Unfortunately, the Swiss Army knife hasn't been recovered," he says. "The pathologist determined that Annie Stone's wounds were consistent with the use of a Swiss Army knife, not the knife that belonged to Bonnie Lambeaux."

"Interesting," I say.

"That's not the only thing that's interesting," he tells me. "Bonnie also, it turns out, has an alibi for the night Annie Stone was killed."

"She does?"

"Bonnie Lambeaux was caught on CCTV wandering around Guavatown at the time the assistant was killed," he says, "between 10 p.m. and 2 a.m. until she finally fell asleep on a park bench."

"You know, Bonnie told me that very same thing," I say.

"Detective François is basically back at square one with this case," says Officer Cuetee.

"What about Lucretia Lux?" I ask. "Does Detective François suspect her? Or the dognapper?"

"I passed along all the info from your anonymous sources," says Officer Cuetee. "But I'm not sure if François acted on any of the tips. I'll let you know. Listen, I need to get going. Maybe tea this weekend?"

"Sounds great," I say.

Once Officer Cuetee and I have disconnected, I study the notes on my legal pad. Now that Chef Bonnie is no longer a suspect, I'm thinking the killer has to be either Lucretia Lux, or whoever dognapped James Mortimer.

And, of course, the problem remains, how do I prove any of my speculations?

I'm not sure right now. What I know is that the information Officer Cuetee gave me is huge, and I need to write a follow-up story before I leave. After firing up my computer again, I type the following headline: THE CHEF DIDN'T DO IT!

Chapter 22

"Good news, Sophia," declares Marty as he paces behind his desk, crushing a squeeze toy between his palms.

My boss buzzed me five minutes ago, demanding that I report to his office. Normally, I would be annoyed and worried, but he called after I'd completed perusing my social media feeds while enjoying tea and donut holes, so I was fine with being summoned.

Giddy with excitement, I say, "Good Morning America called."

Marty looks confused. "No."

"Good Morning Britain?"

Shaking his head, Marty growls, "No."

"Good Morning Caribbean?"

His face reddening to a shade reminiscent of a chili pepper, Marty asks, "What are you talking about? Why would Good Morning America, Britain, or Caribbean call?"

"To book me for a segment," I say. "Because my dog park murder stories are all trending!"

"And that's the good news," says Marty. "You're not getting booked on any morning shows."

"Well, I haven't been booked, so far," I say. "But when I figure out who killed Annie Stone …"

"How's that going?"

"I have several suspects I'm investigating," I tell him. "And a few very good leads."

"Tell me about the suspects and the leads," says Marty.

"Well," I begin, "there is Ms. Lux—"

"And why is she a suspect?" Marty cuts in.

"Annie Stone, the assistant, was blackmailing Ms. Lux."

Marty stops pacing and frowns at me. "And you know this how?"

"Bonnie Lambeaux told me," I say. "And her story was confirmed by an anonymous source who happened to be present when Ms. Lux and Annie Stone argued. Apparently, Annie Stone wanted Ms. Lux to give her a part in the new movie Ms. Lux is producing. Ms. Lux refused. And she also slapped Annie and threatened to kill her."

Marty resumes his pacing. "What did Annie Stone have on Ms. Lux? How was she able to blackmail her?"

"Annie Stone had a video of Ms. Lux kicking her dog," I say. "Apparently, it was an accident. Ms. Lux mistook the dog for a turtle."

Marty scowls. "She mistook a dog for a turtle?"

"It's an odd story," I say. "Anyway, the point is, Annie edited the video to make it look like Ms. Lux kicked her dog on purpose. Then Annie threatened to sell the tape to the media if Ms. Lux didn't pay her."

"So, Lucretia Lux paid until Annie Stone wanted to be in the movie," says Marty.

"Exactly," I say. "Ms. Lux couldn't let that video of her kicking the dog get out. She would have been dragged for filth from one end of the internet to the other."

'Is there any proof that Ms. Lux killed Annie Stone?"

I shake my head. "I haven't found any so far—"

"Have you looked?"

Sheepish, I bite my lip. "Well, not exactly ..."

"Why am I not surprised?" Marty sighs, then asks, "Who else are you looking at as a suspect?"

"The dognapper is also a suspect."

Marty gives me a shrewd glare. "Explain. Expound. Extrapolate."

"You want me to explain, expound, *and* extrapolate?" I ask, seeking clarity. "Or, do you want me to explain or expound or extrapolate? Or—"

"Why is the dognapper also a suspect?" demands Marty, dragging a hand down his face.

"Well, Ms. Lux's driver, Esteban, thinks the Corgi was dognapped," I begin, "And, no, he has no proof, and neither do I, but Ms. Lux also thinks the dog was taken, and I'm inclined to agree, considering how popular and valuable the dog is. After all, you remember I told you he was given to Ms. Lux by the King of England. I'll bet someone will send Ms. Lux a ransom note."

Marty asks, "Did you ask Ms. Lux about the claims that she killed the assistant? Did you question her about being blackmailed by Annie Stone?"

"Well, I was going to ask Ms. Lux about the blackmail," I say. "But I didn't get a chance, and—"

"If you have no proof that the assistant was blackmailing Ms. Lux," says Marty, a pointed edge to his tone. "Then you don't have Ms. Lux's motive for murder."

"I understand that," I say. "However—"

"Look, if what your sources told you is true," says Marty, "then I will agree that the cops should be questioning Ms. Lux. But you need to verify what your sources tell you, Sophia. That's something you don't do. Some source tells you something and you run with it. You must thoroughly investigate every lead, every tip. Never assume the source is credible. Verify. Verify. Verify!"

"Absolutely!" I say, jumping up. "I'm headed off to verify. And hopefully, when I do, I'll be able to determine if my sources were telling the truth."

Chapter 23

Moments later, back at my desk, I sit down, grab a pen and a legal pad.

At the top of the page, I write: TO DO

And below the heading, which I wrote in all capital letters, I write:

1. Verify claims of sources.

And then I write:

2.

And then I take a breath and tap the pen against the paper. What else do I need to do other than verify that the turtle was telling the truth about Ms. Lux slapping Annie Stone and threatening to kill her?

Oh, I know … and I write:

2. Investigate suspects thoroughly

Again, I tap the pen against the legal pad. Question is, how do I verify the turtle's claims? The driver, Esteban, was no help. He insisted that Annie Stone wouldn't have blackmailed Ms. Lux. Of course, I could question Ms. Lux, but would she be honest? Do I expect the A-list, award-winning actress to snitch on herself?

My desk phone rings.

I grab it and answer, "*Palmchat Gazette*, this is Sophie Carter, how can I help you?"

"You wrote that story about the missing dog, right?" asks the caller, a male with a nasal whine that reminds me of annoying sand flies.

"Yes, I did!" I say, then ask, "Are you calling because you have a tip or a lead about the whereabouts of Lucretia Lux's Corgi?"

The man with the nasal whine says, "I'm calling because I have the dog ..."

My mouth drops open.

Did I just hear what I think I heard? Did the caller just say—

"Hello? Are you still there?"

Clearing my throat, I say, "You have the dog?"

"Yes."

"You have James Mortimer?"

"That's what I said."

"You have Lucretia Lux's Corgi? The Corgi given to her by the King of England?"

"Are you hearing impaired?" asks the caller. "Do you have some sort of comprehension deficiency?"

I take a deep breath. "Where is he?"

"I'm not going to tell you."

"You're not? I don't understand," I say. "You called to say you have the dog but you don't want to tell me where he is ..."

"You didn't let me finish," he says. "I called to tell you that I have the dog and I want you to tell Lucretia Lux that if she wants the dog, it's going to cost her."

"You want a ransom for the dog?

"Of course, I want money for the dog," he says. "Not only does the Corgi belong to a wealthy, A-list actress but the dog is royalty, meaning this canine is very valuable. Worth a million dollars, easy."

"You want a million dollars for the dog?"

"You think that's not enough? Maybe I should ask for more? Maybe one-point-five million?"

"I don't think you should hold the dog for ransom," I say, hoping my voice holds enough censure and rebuke to shame the dognapper. "I think you should do the kind and compassionate thing and return the dog to Ms. Lux, who has been wrecked with grief about her missing Corgi."

"Why should I be kind and compassionate to Ms. Lux?" asks the caller. "She's certainly not kind and compassionate. She's a bitter, tyrannical hag!"

"That's a pretty strong opinion for someone you don't even know," I say.

"Who says I don't know Lucretia Lux?"

"Do you know her?"

"No, I don't know her," he says. "But I heard she's a bitter, tyrannical hag."

"You heard?" I ask. "Did someone tell you that?"

"Look, that doesn't matter," says the caller. "The point is Lucretia Lux doesn't deserve kindness or compassion. If you ask me, the dog is better without her."

"Is that why you kidnapped the dog?" I ask, curious. "Were you trying to rescue him? Was he being mistreated, or—"

"First of all, I didn't dognap him," says the caller.

"Did you find him?"

"He was given to me," says the caller.

"Someone gave the Corgi to you?" I'm doubtful of this claim, and thus, as Marty would say, it must be verified. "When? And who gave you the dog?"

"That doesn't matter," he says. "What matters is that I have James Mortimer and if Lucretia Lux wants him back, she needs to give me a million dollars."

"Okay, but, then why are you telling me?" I ask. "Contact Ms. Lux and tell her—"

"I can't do that," he says.

"Why not?"

"Because if I contact Lucretia Lux," says the caller, "and tell her I want a million dollars for the safe return of James Mortimer, she'll agree to my demands—"

"Which is what you want, right?"

"Yes, but, she'll be lying to me," the guy says. "Lucretia will promise to pay me the money and then arrange a meeting place. But when I get to said meeting place, she'll knock me in the head and take the dog without giving me anything."

"Well, yes, I suppose that's possible."

"That's exactly what she'll do," insists the caller.

"But, that's the risk you take when you dognap a Corgi and demand a ransom," I tell him. "Ms. Lux could also have the police waiting to arrest you when you show up at the prearranged meeting place."

"I didn't even think of that, but you're right," he says. "Which is why I want you to facilitate the ransom negotiations and act as a liaison."

I pull the phone from my ear, stare at the receiver, and then put it back to my ear. "Excuse me?"

"I want you to contact Lucretia Lux for me," says the caller. "Tell her I have the dog and give her my ransom demand."

"And if she agrees?" I ask.

"I'll call you back at this same time tomorrow," the dognapper says. "You can tell me if Lucretia will give me the money. If so, I will tell you where to drop the ransom money. When you drop off the money, there will be a note with the location of the dog."

"Listen, I don't think—"

"Look, that's how it's going to go," says the caller. "You want a happy ending to your story, right? You can be the reason that Lucretia Lux and James Mortimer are reunited. What do you say?"

Chapter 24

It's two o'clock in the afternoon, and right about now, I'd love to be enjoying a steaming mug of green tea and cinnamon chai donut holes.

But, I'm not.

I am nowhere close to enjoying tea and donut holes.

Instead, I'm getting suspicious glances, curious glares, and harsh words from Marty, Detective François, and Lucretia Lux.

How, you may ask, is this happening?

Well ... after my conversation with the dognapper, I took a moment, or two—possibly three—to wrap my head around what he confessed to me. And I took another minute, or two—possibly seven —to process his ridiculous plan ...

I want you to facilitate the ransom negotiations and act as a liaison

Naturally, I didn't know how to wrap my head around his confession or process his plan, so I went to Marty. After relaying the conversation with the dognapper to Marty, my boss decided to contact Detective François and Lucretia Lux. The A-list actress and the brooding detective arrived within the hour.

We all went into the conference room, where I relayed my

conversation with the mystery dognapper to Detective François, Lucretia Lux, and Esteban, Ms. Lux's driver.

At present, we're still convened in the large conference room, sitting around the polished, oblong table.

"Ms. Carter," begins the detective, directing a baleful glare at me. "How do you know that the caller really has James Mortimer?"

Marty and Ms. Lux stare at me, waiting, and I swallow, not sure what to say, but managing to come up with, "Well, because he said he had the dog?"

"Did the caller show you proof of life?" asks Detective François.

"Proof of life?" I squeak.

"Did you ask, Sophia?" demands Marty, scratching the brittle spikes of hair sprouting from his scalp.

Clearing my throat, feeling like an idiot, I say, "Well, I, um ... you see—"

"Think back to the conversation with the dognapper," says Detective François. "Do you recall any background noise?"

"Background noise?" I ask, trying to remember.

"Could you tell if the dognapper was calling from an interior or an exterior location?" asks Detective François. "Did you hear any traffic sounds? Did you hear a dog barking?"

Glum, wishing I had paid more attention during the phone call, I shake my head. "I don't remember any background noises. I wish I did, but—"

"It's okay, Sophie," says Lucretia Lux, giving me a sympathetic smile. "I know you did your best under the circumstances, which were no doubt harrowing."

Esteban snorts. "I doubt background noise would have provided the location of the dognapper."

"Actually, the location of the dognapper might have been identified that way," informs the detective. "But, there's still a possibility of determining the location with the newspaper's phone records."

"The guy was probably calling from a burner," says Esteban.

"Most likely he was," agrees the detective. "Nevertheless, we may be able to trace the location of the burner with GPS. If we're able to do that, we can put eyes and ears on the location and rescue the dog."

"Detective François, with all due respect," says Lucretia Lux, "I think the best way to get James Mortimer back is to pay the dognapper, which I am more than willing and able to do."

"So, do I," agrees Esteban.

"Paying the dognapper won't be necessary," says Detective François.

Her face stricken, Lucretia Lux says, "But, what if you can't trace the burner?"

"Then we'll employ Plan B," says Detective François.

"What's Plan B?" asks Marty.

"When the dognapper calls tomorrow," says Detective François, "Ms. Carter will inform him that Ms. Lux has accepted his ransom demands. Then Ms. Carter will get the location of the money drop. Once I have that information, I'll assign officers to the drop location. When the dognapper picks up the money, we'll apprehend him, and rescue the dog."

Wringing her hands, Lucretia Lux asks, "And you're sure that's the best thing to do? What if the dognapper gets suspicious and sends Sophie to a fake drop location, or—"

"Trust me, Ms. Lux," says the detective. "If we don't trace the burner and rescue the dog today, then we'll employ Plan B and rescue him tomorrow. Don't worry."

Standing, Ms. Lux says, "I'll try not to."

"Before you go, Ms. Lux," says Detective François. "I'd like to have a word with you, and Mr. Esteban, in private."

Ms. Lux frowns. "About?"

The detective looks at Marty. "Mind if we use your conference room?"

"Not at all," says Marty, jumping up. "Sophia and I will get out of your way."

Moments later, standing outside the closed conference room, Marty says, "Make sure you ask Ms. Lux and her driver what François wanted to talk to them about."

"Absolutely!" I say, smiling despite the dubious look Marty gives me before he turns and stomps back to his office.

Exhaling, I bite my lip. I'm not sure how long Detective François will take to question Ms. Lux and Esteban. I could go back to my desk and try to get some fact-checking done, but I don't have any facts to check, at the moment. And if I do go back to my desk, I might miss Ms. Lux and Esteban when they leave. I figure, in order not to blow it, the best thing would be to wait outside the conference room.

And so, I walk across the hallway and lean against the wall next to the janitor's closet.

As I wait, my mind drifts to the dognapper. I could kick myself for not paying better attention during the call. Why didn't I listen for background noise? And even more than that, why didn't I question him more thoroughly? Why didn't I demand proof that he actually does have James Mortimer? Why didn't I ask him if he had anything to do with Annie Stone's murder? The more I consider Esteban's theory, the more I think the driver might be right. Maybe Annie Stone was killed while trying to protect the Corgi. And if that's true, then—

The conference room door opens and I jump as Detective François walks out, leaving the door slightly ajar.

Swallowing, I brave his scowl and open my mouth to ask him—

The detective holds up a hand and shakes his head.

Crestfallen, I press my lips together and step back as he passes me, striding down the hall and around the corner, out of sight. Honestly, I don't know why I'm disappointed. Since when has the detective ever given me a statement? I knew he would refuse to—

" … did you tell him?" Lucretia Lux's voice floats from the conference room, arresting my thoughts. Intrigued, I tiptoe across to the slightly opened doors to listen.

"I didn't say anything," whispers Esteban.

"Are you sure?" demands Lucretia.

"I swear—"

"Then how did that detective find out?" Lucretia asks.

Stammering Esteban says, "I don't know. I promise I have no idea."

Clapping a hand over my mouth to prevent a gasp from escaping, I realize what Detective François wanted to question Lucretia Lux about.

"Who else could have told François about me slapping Annie and threatening her?" asks Lucretia. "No one else knows that happened except me and you. And I certainly didn't tell him!"

"Look, I don't know how he found out," swears Esteban. "You told me not to say anything and I didn't."

"Esteban, if I find out that you didn't keep your mouth shut," says Lucretia, her tone low and menacing. "You will be sorry. Do you understand me?"

"Yes, Ms. Lux," says Esteban, his voice quavering. "I understand—"

"Do not cross me," says Lucretia. "Don't make the same mistake Annie did, okay? You know what happened to her. Don't think that I won't get rid of you … just like I got rid of her …"

Esteban mumbles a reply, one I can't make out, but that might be because I'm too busy trying to process the fact that I think Ms. Lux just threatened to kill him. But, that can't be right, can it? I must have heard wrong. Or, maybe misunderstood what I heard. Or—

"Ms. Carter?"

Jolted from my thoughts, I blink.

Lucretia Lux is standing in front of me, gaping at me with wide, confused eyes. "What are you doing here?

Startled, I stumble over my words. "Oh, yes, um, right, well, you see—"

"Oh, yes, um, right, well, you see what?" demands Esteban, giving me a suspicious glare.

Worried that he might suspect I was eavesdropping, I clear my throat. "I was just coming to find you to let you know, Ms. Lux, that I think Detective François' plan will work out, so you don't have to worry."

"Thank you for your help with this awful situation," says Ms. Lux, taking my hand as she gives me a grateful smile. She seems so compassionate and understanding. Her tone is kind and melodic. She appears and sounds nothing like the woman I overheard promising to get rid of Esteban if he dared to cross her.

Ms. Lux continues, "It's very brave of you to risk dealing with a vicious dognapper. I agree that the detective's plan will work and James Mortimer will be rescued."

As Lucretia Lux and Esteban walk away, I'm gobsmacked and conflicted, struggling to reconcile the kind, A-list actress with the woman who might have just confessed to killing Annie Stone.

With a weary exhale, I head to the breakroom.

I need tea and sympathy. But, mainly, just tea. Sympathy is nice, but nothing beats a steaming mug of elderberry and jasmine tea for relaxation and pensive reflection.

And I have much to reflect on.

Namely, do I tell the police what I overheard Lucretia Lux say to

Esteban? That she got rid of Annie Stone and she would get rid of him, too, if he tried to cross her? Would the police believe me? Detective François already questioned Lucretia about slapping and threatening Annie Stone, which she no doubt denied. But, if I tell him what I heard, then he could catch Lucretia in a lie.

But, then again, he might dismiss my information as hearsay. After all, I have no proof of what Lucretia said to Esteban. She would deny saying it, and I'm inclined to believe that Esteban would corroborate her lies.

Chapter 25

"The Dumb Cluck Chicken Shack," says the dognapper with the nasal whine.

As promised, he called the same time today as he did yesterday.

As directed by Detective François, I told the dognapper that Ms. Lux had accepted his terms and asked him for the location of the money drop.

"Do you know that place?" asks the dognapper.

"The Dumb Luck Chicken Cluck?" I repeat, not exactly sure I've heard of the establishment.

"No, the Dumb Cluck Chicken Shack," he corrects.

"Dumb Cluck Chicken Shack," I say. "Um. Yeah. Sure. I think."

"Well, that's where I want you to leave the money," he says. "Ask to be seated at table eight. Order the fried chicken tender platter with sweet potato fries, black beans, and extra papaya sauce."

"Does it have to be papaya sauce?" I ask. "I prefer mango."

"They don't have mango," he says. "But they have guava. Or you might try the passionfruit sauce."

"Can I try both?" I ask. "They sound quite tasty."

"I think so," he says. "After you finish the meal, leave the duffel bag under the table and leave. After I get the money and count it, I'll call you and give you the location of the dog."

"Sounds like a plan," I say. "Oh, before you go … I need proof of life of the dog. Ms. Lux is demanding that."

"I'll email you a video," he says.

"Great," I say, then give him my email address at the *Palmchat Gazette*. "What time should I arrive at the restaurant?"

"Six o'clock this evening," he says and then hangs up.

With excitement and trepidation racing through my veins, I jump up and run to Marty's office.

"The dognapper called," I announce, and then repeat the details of the conversation.

"Let's call François," says Marty, picking up the receiver on his desk phone. Moments later, when the detective is on the line, Marty presses the Speaker button and I inform François about my call with the dognapper.

"Did he tell you where to leave the money?" demands François.

"Yes, he did," I say.

"Where's the drop location?" asks François.

At once, I'm hesitant for some reason, and then it occurs to me that I don't quite remember the location of the money drop. At least, I don't think I remember. But maybe I do. Or maybe—

"Sophia!" barks Marty.

Jumping in my seat, I clear my throat. "Um … it's a restaurant."

"What restaurant?" asks Marty, scowling at me, his face starting to look like a steamed lobster.

"Please don't hate me," I say. "I think the name of the restaurant had the word cluck."

"You think it had the word cluck?" Marty is livid. "You didn't write it down?"

Detective François says, "Must mean the Joy Cluck Chicken Club."

"That's right," I agree, even though, technically, I'm not sure. "Absolutely! That was it! The Joy Cluck Chicken Club."

Slumping in his creaky leather chair, Marty shakes his head.

"And what time are you to make the money drop?" asks François.

"Six o'clock this evening," I say.

"Are you sure?" asks Marty, giving me a dubious look.

"Absolutely!" I confirm. "He wants me to order the fried chicken nugget platter ... no, wait, I'm supposed to order the fried chicken tender platter, and—"

"What does it matter what you order?"

"I'm not sure," I confess. "But I'm looking forward to trying the passionfruit dipping sauce. Normally, I prefer mango sauce with chicken tenders, but—"

"Sophia, please stay focused," instructs Marty.

"What happens after you order the food?" asks the detective.

"After I finish the meal," I say, "he wants me to leave the duffel bag of cash under the table—I have to request table eight—"

"Why table eight?"

"I'm not sure," I admit, wishing I'd asked.

"And then?"

"And then he'll get the duffle bag, count the money, and then call me with the location of the Corgi," I say. "Oh, and ... I got proof of life. Well, the dognapper is emailing me the proof that James Mortimer is alive."

"Forward that email to me," says the detective. "I'll get our IT department to track the IP address. We may have his location before you show up at the restaurant."

"That would be great," I say, anxious to get back to my desk and check my email.

François asks, "Ms. Carter, you are acquainted with Officer Noah Cuetee, correct?"

"Yes, I am," I say. "He's my ... um, friend."

I'm thankful I caught myself before spilling the beans about Office Cuetee being my confidential police source.

The detective says, "Officer Cuetee will join you at the Joy Cluck Chicken Club, but the two of you won't be together. He'll be in plain clothes. After you leave, he'll remain at the restaurant to apprehend the dog thief once he takes possession of the ransom money."

"Sounds like a plan," I say.

"I'll be in touch," says the detective before disconnecting the call.

Glancing at Marty, I squeal in exhilarated anticipation. "Isn't this exciting? I'm going to be part of a police sting operation!"

"And that's the part I don't particularly like," says Marty, rubbing his jaw.

"What part is that?"

"The part about you joining a police operation, Sophia," says Marty, with an annoyed exhale.

"What don't you like about that part?" I ask.

"It's dangerous," says Marty. "I can't believe François would agree to let you take part in the money drop."

"Probably because the dognapper wanted it that way," I say. "If we don't at least pretend that we're going along with his demands, then we'll never rescue James Mortimer. And we'll never find Annie Stone's killer, who may or may not be the dognapper. Now I'm not sure because …"

"Because?"

"Because Lucretia Lux might have killed Annie Stone."

Marty nods. "Because the assistant was blackmailing her about kicking the dog."

"Well, that's not the only reason I think Lucretia might have killed Annie Stone," I confide.

"What's the other reason?"

"Lucretia might have confessed to the murder," I say.

Marty scowls at me. "What?"

I tell Marty the conversation I overheard between Ms. Lux and Esteban, then ask, "You think I should question Ms. Lux about what I heard?"

Scratching the thin, spiky stubble on his chin, Marty shakes his head. "She'll just deny saying it. Or, tell you that you misheard, or misunderstood."

I nod. "You're probably right."

"Instead, wait until François arrests the dognapper. I'm sure the detective will be able to get the truth from the him. If François determines that the dognapper didn't kill Annie Stone, then you can pivot and focus your investigation on Lucretia Lux."

"Sounds like a plan," I say

"Speaking of plans," says Marty. "As I said, I don't like this sting operation. Despite what you told me about Ms. Lux, she might be innocent. This dognapper could very well have killed Annie Stone. So … be careful."

"Are you worried about me?" I ask, wondering if that was a hint of concern in Marty's gruff tone.

"What? Worried about you?" Marty scowls. "Don't be ridiculous. On second thought, I am worried—that you'll blow it. So try your best not to, Sophia. Remember. You're still on probation. I will ship you out if you don't shape up!"

Chapter 26

"Girl, this place is a dump!" declares Callie, rising on her hind legs, stretching her body to lean over the dashboard.

"Well, no, it's not Morsure de Requin," I say, referencing one of St. Mateo's most exclusive fine dining restaurants, the name of which means "shark bite" in English. "But it's not as bad as the Crusty Crab-n-Clam Bake. Now that place is a dump."

"Looks just as bad to me," says the cat, settling back down onto the passenger seat. "I don't think I want to go in."

"Callie …" I whine, pulling into an available parking space. "You have to!"

I need the Calico's support now more than ever. I was thrilled when I walked out to my JEEP and heard Callie's now familiar greeting: *Hey, sis …*

Following greetings and a bit of catch-up, I told the cat about the sting operation to catch the dognapper. As she's never been a fan of sting operations, Callie wasn't happy, but she found some comfort in the fact that Detective François and the cops were involved.

She sensed my apprehension, however, and when I begged her to join me, she agreed.

"You can't let me go in alone," I tell the feline. "You promised to do this with me."

Licking her fur, Callie stares at me. "You do look as nervous as a fly caught in a spider's web."

"I am," I tell her.

My excitement about the sting operation turned to apprehension as the time passed and when five o'clock rolled around, I was a mess of fear and anxiety. I worried Marty was right and maybe taking part in a dangerous sting operation was too risky.

And what if the dog thief was a murdering fiend? If the dognapper had killed Annie Stone, he wouldn't hesitate to kill me too.

And then I was afraid I would blow the sting operation somehow. Maybe I would accidentally or inadvertently do something suspicious and scare off the dognapper. I guessed that while I ate, the dog thief would be somewhere nearby, hiding, watching, waiting for me to leave. What if he suspected I was working with the police? He might flee and, because of me, James Mortimer would remain in captivity.

Or, suppose, he took the money, counted it, and refused to return the Corgi. Perhaps, he'd become attached to the dog and didn't want to give him up ... sort of like in the way I've become attached to Callie.

"Girl, are you sure they allow cats in that place?"

"According to the website," I say, cutting the ignition, "all animals are welcome."

"All animals?" The cat stares at me. "Even sand crabs?"

"I think so," I say, reaching into the backseat to grab my oversized bag.

"Girl, I definitely am not going in there if they welcome sand crabs," announces Callie. "A sand crab tried to bite me a few days ago when I was hanging out with the tomcat. I do not trust those little—"

"Callie ..." I warn.

"Alright, alright," says the cat, jumping into my lap. "But you owe me, sis!"

Ten minutes later, I find out that Callie was right.

The Joy Cluck Chicken Club is a dump.

But there's a reason for that. Per the website, at the Joy Cluck Chicken Club, wild chickens roam freely, and patrons are invited to catch the chicken they want the chef to cook if they want the meal for free. As a result, the old, converted barn is overrun with wild chickens, squawking, and shedding feathers and pecking at the feed scattered all over the wood plank floor.

As I walk to the hostess counter, I wrinkle my nose. The place smells like a stuffy chicken coop. The large barn doors are open, but the sea breeze doesn't help the dank humidity.

"I'm going to need a bath once we leave here," announces Callie, trotting alongside me. "And you know how cats feel about water."

"Yeah, you and me both," I say, taking care to avoid the chicken droppings.

The hostess greets me with a smile and a cheery greeting. "Welcome to the Joy Cluck Chicken Club where we hope you'll experience joy and consider yourself clucky when you taste our wonderful chicken!"

"Thank you," I say. "Um … I'd like a table for two."

The hostess frowns. "For two? Will someone be joining you later?"

"Oh, no … I have a friend …" I point at the cat.

"Oh! Welcome, kitty …" says the hostess, starting to bend down.

"Girl, is she about to pet me?" asks the cat, taking a step back. "You better tell her to back off, or—"

"She's not in the mood to be petted today," I say quickly.

"You better let her know, sis," says Callie, licking her fur.

"Oh, I understand," says the hostess, moving back behind the counter.

"So, I was hoping to get table eight," I say, hoping no one has already been seated there. Now that I'm at the restaurant, it occurs to me that I don't know what to do if table eight isn't available. Will it matter to the dognapper if I'm seated at a different table? Or is there something special about table eight? If he doesn't see me sitting at table eight, will he get upset and—

"Right this way," says the hostess, grabbing a menu.

As Callie and I follow the hostess to table eight, I glance around, looking for Officer Cuetee, wondering if he's already here. The place bustling with customers, a large majority of them hooting and hollering as they dash around, trying to catch chickens. I have to duck and dodge both man and foul as we navigate through the wooden picnic tables.

After we're seated, the hostess informs us that our server will be with us.

Callie jumps onto the table.

"Sis, please don't tell me you're going to eat anything in this joint," says Callie as she glances around.

"Well ..." I pick up the menu and lower my head, trying to talk to the cat without drawing attention to myself. "I have to order the chicken tender platter."

"Girl, whatever," says Callie, licking her paw. "This place looks like a health hazard. I'm surprised it hasn't been—"

A chicken lands on our table.

Gasping, I shriek.

"Get lost!" Callie hisses and bats a paw against the chicken's beak.

Squawking, the chicken steps toward Callie.

"I wish you would try to peck my eyes out!" Callie hisses again. "I will pluck out every last one of those dirty feathers!"

"Shoo!" I say to the chicken, who seems determined to get in the feline's face. "Go away!"

"Gotcha!" cries a man as he leaps toward table eight, arms outstretched, and grabs the chicken.

"Look at you," Callie taunts the chicken, who squawks furiously as the man struggles to hold on to it. "Got caught slipping! Now you're going to end up in the deep fryer!"

"Callie …" I admonish.

The cat gives me a look. "Girl, you know it's true."

Callie's right. But, I'm not sure this particular chicken will end up in the deep fryer, as it seems to be fighting for its life. And it seems to be a fight the chicken might win, considering how it's pecking at the man's face and clawing his neck with it's rough, spindly feet.

"Sophie …"

Recognizing the voice, I glance to my right.

Officer Cuetee is standing next to table eight, looking cuter than I've ever seen him look, and trust me, I've seen him looking pretty good. He is a certified dreamboat, as my grandma would say. And as much as I'd like to stare at him and swoon, I can't. His presence—and the duffle bag he's holding—reminds me that I'm not here to figure out which sauce would taste better with my chicken tenders, the guava, or the passionfruit.

I'm at the Joy Luck Chicken Club to help nab a dognapper.

"You okay?" asks Officer Cuetee.

"What is he saying?" demands Callie. "Is he wondering why I'm here? If he is, tell him, so am I. Wait, no, tell him that my human forced me to—"

"I'm good," I say, giving the cat a quick eye roll. "How are you?"

"Ready to catch this dognapper," says Officer Cuetee.

"So am I," I say. "I'm just hoping I don't blow it."

"Why would you blow it?" he asks, concern in his gorgeous blue eyes.

Shrugging, I say, "I just don't want to mess things up. I want everything to go smoothly, so I'll have a great first-person account article, one that will trend."

Officer Cuetee gives me an adorable smile. "I'm sure you'll do fine. You have the easy part. You just have to babysit this duffle bag and then leave. I have to follow the dognapper, make sure he doesn't notice me, and then arrest him."

Nodding, I ask, "Does François think the dognapper killed Annie Stone?"

"Not sure," says Officer Cuetee. "I think he thinks it's a possibility."

"What about Lucretia Lux?" I ask. "Does François suspect her?"

"Maybe," says Officer Cuetee. "I gave him the tip from your anonymous source about Annie Stone blackmailing Ms. Lux."

"François questioned her about that when he, Lucretia, and her driver came to the paper to discuss the sting operation," I say. "I'm sure she denied being blackmailed, but ..."

"But?" prompts Officer Cuetee.

"After François left, I overheard Lucretia Lux talking to Esteban," I say. "She accused him of telling the cops about her slapping and threatening Annie Stone. He denied it. And then Lucretia told him not to cross her or she'd get rid of him like she got rid of Annie Stone."

Officer Cuetee frowns. "Are you serious?"

"You think I should tell François?" I ask. "I have no proof of their conversation."

"I still think he should know," says Officer Cuetee.

Nodding, I say, "Maybe if you tell him, he'll be more inclined to—"

"Nobody move!" The harsh, booming command reverberates

throughout the barn. "Everybody put your hands up! Now! Move and it will be the last thing you do!"

Chapter 27

The restaurant erupts into a cacophony of squawking and shouting as the restaurant customers, waitstaff, and all the animals realize what's happening …

I was confused for a hot minute, too, but as I saw Officer Cuetee's face transform from adorable to apprehensive, I realized that the Joy Cluck Chicken Club is being robbed.

"Girl, I'm getting out of here," says Callie, "and I suggest you do too!"

"I can't …" I whisper from the corner of my mouth, watching to make sure Officer Cuetee is concentrating on the robbers, and not staring at me as I talk to a cat. "I have to do the sting operation."

"Sis, the place is being held up," says Callie, hissing at me. "Stay here if you want to, but I'm not taking a bullet for you!"

"Callie!" I whisper through gritted teeth, but the cat ignores me.

Slinking from her seat to the floor, she slips under the table and stands near my foot.

Bending over slightly, I stare at her. "Thought you were leaving …"

"So did I, but you need me," says Callie.

Grateful that the cat decided to stick around, I glance at Officer Cuetee. He gives me an assuring nod, but I can see the tension and trepidation on his face. Staring at the robbers, a trio of men dressed as Santa's elves, with red and green ski masks, I can't help thinking they could not have picked a worse time to rob the restaurant.

Granted, there's never a good time to rob a restaurant, but Officer Cuetee and I are in the middle of a sting operation. Sighing, I watch the elves, armed with guns and toy sacks, move from table to table, demanding money, and valuables. I'm hoping someone can secretly alert the police, although I know if the cops come, then the dognapper won't show up.

"Listen, sis," says Callie. "I got a plan …"

Worried, I bend over, pretending I'm going to tie my shoe, even though I'm not wearing shoes with strings. Beneath the table, Callie and three chickens congregate.

"What is going on?" I whisper.

"Me and these chicks are going to handle the robbers," says Callie.

"What? How? No, Callie, please, don't do anything dangerous!" I plead. "I'm sure the cops are on the way!"

But the cat isn't listening.

She's slinking away from the table, maneuvering beneath the next table over, followed by the chickens. Raising up, I catch Officer Cuetee's eye.

"What is it?" he asks.

"I think my cat is going to do something crazy," I say, craning my neck, looking for Callie and watching the robbers, who are making their way toward table eight.

"Something crazy? Like what?" asks Officer Cuetee. "Wait. I thought you didn't have a cat."

"You know, the cat I know?" I ask. "She's got some dangerous plan."

"Dangerous plan? How do you know that?"

Arrested by the skepticism in his tone, I bite my lip. "Well, she … had that look in her eyes that she had when she attacked me, so—"

A hissing howl splits the atmosphere, causing confusion and commotion.

A second later, Callie leaps from the edge of one of the tables, flying through the air, and sinks her claws into the ski mask of one of the robbers. Scratching, clawing, and biting, she attacks with ferocious intensity as the robber screams in shock, dropping his gun.

At the same time, his startled friends are beset by flying chickens, who roost on their heads and shoulders, and commence pecking at the ski masks.

"Get these angry birds off me!" shouts one of the larcenous elves, trying to shoo the chickens away.

"Help!" shouts the third robber, flailing and twirling around. "My eyes! My eyes!" Banging against a table, he loses his balance and falls to the floor. Promptly, several customers surround him and proceed to goat tie him with a collection of belts donated by a few of the diners.

Officer Cuetee drops the duffle bag and springs into action, grabbing the second robber.

A waitress picks up the dropped gun, points it at the robber still wrestling with Callie, and tells him not to move or she'll put a dozen holes in him.

"Callie!" I scream over the chaotic melee.

Releasing her hold on the man, who slumps to the floor, landing in a puddle of fresh chicken poop, Callie leaps across several tables until she's back at table eight.

"Callie, you were so great!" I tell her, as the sounds of sirens grow louder.

"Girl, I know," says the cat, stretching out on the table. "Just make sure that when you write the article, you get the facts straight. I came up with the plan. And make sure you spell my name right. Callie with two 'L's and an 'E' at the end."

Chapter 28

"Did it really all go down like that?" asks Clark, taking a sip of coffee.

"Absolutely!" I say, taking a sip of my rosemary, blood orange, and hibiscus tea.

"Are you sure, Sophie?" asks Candace, sipping water and giving me a dubious glance.

It's two in the afternoon, and the three of us are taking a break as we discuss my article, which I wrote two days ago: ANIMALS TO THE RESCUE AFTER CHICKEN SHACK ROBBED. The article was lively and fun to write, and it trended well, with hundreds of comments from animal lovers.

Unfortunately, it wasn't the article I planned to write.

As suspected, the robbers and the cops—or, the cops and robbers, if you prefer—scared away the dognapper, who never showed up, even though Officer Cuetee and I stuck around long after the customers had given statements and were released to leave.

Thankfully, no one blamed me, but I still felt like a failure. Nevertheless, I am determined to complete the sting operation and do my part to help catch the dognapper. Now all the dognapper has to do is call me. I would contact him, but the number he called me from was a burner, according to the cops. And the email he used to send the proof of life video of James Mortimer had an IP registered to an internet café where patrons could pay to use public computers. Detective François sent Officer Cuetee to the internet café to find out the identity of the dognapper, but the proprietor only accepted cash and wasn't the type to pay attention to his customers. In any event, the crime scene techs took fingerprints, but Officer Cuetee told me he's doubtful they'll get a hit on some crook in the criminal database since the café owner disinfects the computer keyboards after each use.

"Yes, Candace, I'm sure," I tell her. "I was there, remember?"

"True, but were you paying attention?" asks Candace. "Or, while trying not to be robbed or shot, did you look away and miss some details."

"I didn't miss any details."

After another sip of water, Candace says, "Your article suggested that the cat led the charge against the robbers."

"She did," I say, remembering Callie's fierce bravery, which made me super proud.

"And it was the cat that's not your cat," confirms Clark. "The cat who put you in a coma."

"She didn't put me in a coma," I remind Clark. "But, yes, the cat I know."

"Why did you take the cat to the restaurant?" asks Candace.

"I needed a little moral support," I say.

"So she's a support cat?" asks Candace.

"I wouldn't say that," I say. "But I was certainly glad that she was there."

"What about the sting operation?" Clark asks.

"Hopefully, it will still happen," I say. "It's on hold for now. But as soon as the dognapper contacts me again, I'll be ready to do my part to help rescue James Mortimer."

Chapter 29

Fifteen minutes later, back at my desk, as I sit down to fact-check a few articles, my desk phone rings.

A surge of electric adrenaline shoots through me. The dognapper, I think, my heart thumping. It has to be him, calling to make arrangements for me to drop off the ransom money, which I assume will be at a different location. Excited by the opportunity to complete the sting operation, I grab the phone.

"Hello …" I say, my voice a bit breathless.

"Sophia Carter, please," says a brisk, efficient, and yet ebullient female voice.

"This is she," I say, disappointed. I was hoping to hear the nasal whine.

"My name is Edith Fong," the woman tells me. "I work at the St. Felipe Furry Friends Animal Rescue Center."

My interest piqued, I ask, "How can I help you, Ms. Fong?"

"Well, I apologize for not calling sooner," she begins. "I meant to phone you a few weeks ago, but we've been busy trying to place dozens of goats with foster families."

"You place goats with foster families?" I ask.

"Oh, yes," she says, her voice airy and cheerful. "People love to give their kids a kid, but when it grows up to be a nanny or a Billy goat, the children lose interest."

"Odd," I say. "You'd think they would want to keep the goat for the grass."

"We do point that out as an advantage," says Ms. Fong. "And of course, eventually, you can always turn the goat into stew, or tenders, or chops."

"Right …" I say, though I'm not sure a family would want to eat their pet goat.

"Anyway, I'm calling because we received a call from the St. Mateo shelter about a Calico cat named Callie," says Ms. Fong. "One of the workers there, Bev Moore, said you were supposed to call our shelter to ask about the person who adopted Callie."

"Yes, yes," I say, remembering. "But I'm not sure if I was able to call the shelter. Or, if I did, I can't remember if I spoke to anyone."

"I don't think you called," says Ms. Fong. "Or, maybe you did but I didn't get the message. We have lots of volunteers and, unfortunately, too much disorganization. We have protocols, but people like to do things their own way, and sometimes, information gets lost in the ether. Nevertheless, after I talked to Bev about your Calico, I remembered her."

"So you know who adopted Callie?" I ask.

"Callie wasn't adopted by anyone," says Ms. Fong.

"I don't understand."

"Bev misremembered your Calico," says Ms. Fong. "She told you about a sickly little Calico kitten who was found with a litter of four siblings, right?"

"That's right," I say. "Or … was that wrong?"

"Those five Calico kittens were all adopted by an elderly couple with a horse farm," says Ms. Fong. "All five still live with the couple.

Your cat was a different Calico that showed up at the shelter months later."

"So, was she surrendered to the shelter?" I ask, sickened by the thought of someone giving Callie away because they no longer wanted her.

Ms. Fong says, "Actually, it was worse than that."

Wary, I ask, "What do you mean?"

"Your Calico was abandoned in the shelter's parking lot in the middle of the night."

"What?" I ask, shocked.

"Fortunately, the exterior camera surveillance recorded the incident," says Ms. Fong. "A car pulls into the parking lot. With the car still running, the door opens and someone gets out—we could never figure out if it was a man or a woman. The person opened the back door, reached in, and took out a cat carrier, which he, or she, left on the ground. Then the person got back into the car and drove away."

"That's terrible."

"Good thing was when they drove off, the license plate was visible," she says. "We were able to give the license information to the police."

"So you found out who abandoned Callie?"

"Yes … and no," says Ms. Fong.

"What do you mean?"

"Well … it was odd," she says. "The license plate was registered to a car that belong to a man named Walter Wagner."

"Walter Wagner," I repeat, grabbing a pen and legal pad to write down the name. Walter Wagner. Could he be Callie's owner? And, if so, why would he abandon the feisty feline at an animal shelter in the middle of the night?

"The problem was," begins Ms. Fong, "that the Walter Wagner who owned the car in the surveillance video was … dead."

"Dead?"

"So, obviously, Walter Wagner wasn't driving that car," says Ms. Fong.

"Maybe the car was stolen?"

"The police suggested that," she says, "but the car wasn't reported stolen."

"Did the police contact Walter Wagner's family?"

"Apparently, he didn't have any family," says Ms. Fong. "The cops talked to his neighbors. They knew him as a man who lived alone and never had any visitors. But, and here's what I find mysterious, the neighbors who knew him all said that he didn't have a cat."

"That is mysterious," I agree, scribbling notes on the legal pad.

"Another good thing, I thought, at least," she says, "was that when the police viewed the surveillance video, they were able to enhance it, and determined that the person driving the car had been wearing a Hullabaloo Coffee Shop hat. I was thinking the person might have worked there, but ..."

"But?"

"The police weren't interested in following up on that lead," says Ms. Fong. "They suggested that we should come to terms with not knowing who abandoned the Calico and just try to find her a home."

"But, you said she wasn't adopted, right?"

"No, Callie wasn't adopted," says Ms. Fong. "Callie ... disappeared."

A shiver passes through me. "Disappeared?"

"For months, she was at the shelter," Ms. Fong says. "And then one day, she was gone..."

Chapter 30

With an elbow propped on my desk, I stare at the telephone.

I ended the call with Ms. Fong ten minutes ago, but I can't stop thinking about what she told me. The idea of Callie disappearing from the shelter is curious and worrisome. What could have happened to her? How could she have disappeared?

Ms. Fong elaborated at my request, explaining that during a routine morning animal inventory check, Callie's cage was empty. It wasn't open and didn't appear to have been tampered with. Ms. Fong and her staff along with several volunteers searched the shelter, inside and out. But they didn't find Callie.

Even more mysterious was the fact that the surveillance camera system was offline, which it had been for the entire week before Callie's disappearance. The shelter had been waiting for funds from sponsors to get the cameras fixed.

Meaning, someone took Callie when the cameras were down.

I can't help thinking it was an inside job, which Ms. Fong suggested. Only a staff member, or a volunteer, would know that the surveillance wasn't working. And only a staff member or volunteer would have access to the animal cages.

Exhaling, I lean back in my chair.

So far, my quest to find Callie's real owner has been a bust. She was microchipped, but I'm starting to think whoever chipped her gave a fake name and address. Her owner doesn't live in Pebble Republic and his name is not Sebastian Smith. Neither is her owner Walter Wagner. He's dead, and when he was alive, he didn't own a cat. But someone used Wagner's car to abandon Callie at the shelter in St. Felipe.

Who did that? And why? And where is that person now?

More importantly, how do I find out?

I need a different opinion. Clark, I think, and jump up. I'll go down to his cubicle, tell him about the phone call from the shelter, and ask him what he thinks about—

The desk phone rings again.

Slightly distracted, I grab the phone and answer it. "Sophie Carter. How can I help you?"

"Where were you yesterday?"

"Excuse me?"

"We were supposed to meet at the Dumb Cluck Chicken Shack," the caller says. "Why didn't you show up?"

At once, I recognize the nasal whine.

It's the dognapper! I've been waiting on pins and needles for his call, and now he's on the phone, and yet I'm confused because I did show up at the restaurant.

"I was there," I tell him. "You didn't show up, not surprisingly, after the place got robbed."

"The Dumb Cluck Chicken Shack was robbed? When? Not when I was there," he says.

"When were you there?"

"At six o'clock," he insists. "I was waiting for you to come, watching from the shadows. I waited two hours and you didn't show up."

"You couldn't have been waiting in the shadows at the Joy Cluck Chicken Club at six o'clock," I tell him.

"I wasn't waiting in the shadows at the Joy Cluck Chicken Club," he says, "I was at the Dumb Cluck Chicken Shack."

Perplexed, I ask, "Why were you at the Dumb Cluck Chicken Shack?"

"Because that's where you were supposed to leave the ransom money!"

"What? It was?" I ask, trying to remember. "Are you sure?"

"Yes, I'm sure!"

"Oh, I'm sorry," I say, mentally kicking myself. As Marty predicted, I absolutely blew it. "I got the name of the restaurant wrong. I thought you said Joy Cluck Chicken Club. But, listen … Ms. Lux still wants her dog, obviously, and I'm sure you still want the ransom money so … can we try again?"

"Well, that's why I'm calling," he says. "But I don't want you to leave the money at the Joy Cluck Chicken Club."

"You don't?"

"I propose a new location," he says. "I want you to drop the money off at my apartment."

Shocked, I ask, "Your apartment?"

"I know it's risky," he says. "I know you might be tempted to alert the cops, but if you do, Ms. Lux will never see her precious Corgi again and it will be all your fault."

"You're probably right, but …"

"But …"

Hesitating, I bite my lip. I don't have a duffle bag of money to drop off at the dognapper's apartment. But, if I tell the dognapper that, he'll probably end the call. He'll have no use for me if I can't get the ransom money to him.

Of course, I could—and probably should—call Detective François and tell him that the dognapper reached out with new demands.

Problem is, François will never take my call. And, even if he would, the dognapper warned me not to call the police. Of course, if I remember correctly—and it's possible that I don't—the dognapper didn't want the police involved when he told me to leave the money at the Dumb Cluck Chicken Shack, but still I contacted the cops and—

"Hello? Are you still there?"

Startled from my ruminations, I clear my throat. "Yes, of course, I'm still here."

"Well … are you bringing the money to my place, or not?"

My best bet, even though it is risky and probably against my better judgement, is not to tell the dognapper that I don't have any money to drop.

Yes, I'll be lying to him, but it's not like he's a paragon of virtue. The guy stole a dog and he's holding the poor canine for ransom.

And yes, I know I shouldn't be doing my own modified sting operation by myself. I've attempted to do my own sting operations in the past, and they've never worked out the way I planned. They were disasters. And, yes, I could have been killed. But I wasn't. And, not only was I not murdered, but each time, I was able to help catch the killer.

I have a chance to catch another killer tonight.

Annie Stone's killer.

Maybe. Possibly.

Esteban, Ms. Lux's driver, theorized that the killer was the dognapper, and he might be right. Of course, he also might be wrong. Lucretia Lux might have killed her assistant. I can't forget that she admitted to getting rid of Annie Stone. What else could the actress have meant other than she'd stabbed Annie to death?

But back to the dognapper.

If Lucretia didn't kill Annie, then it had to have been the dognapper.

Which means I should probably call Detective François anyway, whether he'll believe me, or not. Or, if not the detective, then I should call Officer Cuetee. And I would absolutely do that if I didn't think Officer Cuetee would advise me against meeting with the dognapper. And I do think he'll tell me not to meet the dognapper.

But, I have to try to get James Mortimer back.

Now, how I'll get the dog back, I'm not quite sure at the moment.

I am somewhat confident, however, that I will come up with a plan. Whether, or not, that plan will work, I have no idea considering that I don't know what the plan is yet, but …

"Okay, I'll come to your apartment," I say. "What's the address …"

Chapter 31

"Girl, whoever dognapped that Corgi hid him very well," says Callie, licking her foot as she settles into the passenger seat of my JEEP. "Nobody knows where he is."

After leaving work for the day, I walked out to the parking lot and found the Calico in her familiar place. Waiting for me on the hood of my vehicle.

"So you haven't had any luck locating James Mortimer?" I ask, steering the JEEP onto the main boulevard. "None of your furry friends have heard anything about a missing Corgi?"

"Girl, did I stutter?" inquires the cat. "No shade, but maybe you should get your hearing checked."

"I was afraid you would say that."

Callie asks, "You were afraid I'd say you need your hearing checked?"

"No, no …" I let out a sigh. "I was afraid you would tell me you haven't found James Mortimer. I was hoping you had, or at least could give me a clue or lead on his whereabouts, so that I wouldn't have to …"

"You wouldn't have to … what?"

"Do my own sting operation."

"Girl, are you serious?"

As I brake to stop at the red traffic light, I glance at the cat. I'm not surprised she's looking at me like I don't have the sense God gave a goat.

"Look, I know my sting operations haven't gone well in the past, but I think I can make this one work."

"Sis, you know the definition of crazy, right?" asks the cat. "Doing the same dumb thing over and over but expecting a different result."

Exhaling, I say nothing, possibly because the cat is right and I have no way to refute her.

"What makes you think you can pull off the sting operation this time?"

"Okay, so, technically, I don't know if I can pull it off," I say, driving through the intersection. "But I have to try."

"Why do you have to try?"

"Because someone dognapped Ms. Lux's Corgi," I say. "I know how that feels."

"Girl, you don't have a dog."

"And I don't have a cat, either," I tell her. "But, when you were catnapped, I was willing to do anything to find you, and I did, so I'd like to help Ms. Lux."

The cat says, "Well, since you insist on carrying out hair-brained schemes, tell me, sis, what's the plan?"

"The plan?"

"You're doing this sting operation to rescue him, right?"

Hesitating, I say, "Um, well, yes … right."

"So, how are you going to rescue him, sis?"

"Well … you see … "

"You don't know, do you?"

"Not exactly, but …" I make a right turn onto another dirt road, following the GPS instructions. "I figure, the dognapper thinks I'm bringing him the ransom money, right?"

"Girl, if you say so …"

"Maybe I could tell him the money is in my JEEP," I say. "The point is to get the dognapper out of his house and then you can go into his house—"

"Girl, did I ask for a part in this plan?" asks the cat, staring at me.

"I need your help, Callie," I tell her.

Licking her paw, the cat hisses. "Yeah, I guess you do. There's no telling what will happen if you do this on your own."

"Things will go sideways without you," I tell Callie. "They'll go inside, outside, upside down."

"Give it a rest, sis," advises the cat. "You already convinced me. You need me."

Expelling a relieved sigh, I say, "Good. Because we're five minutes away from the dognapper's house."

Chapter 32

As the cat and I approach the porch, a shiver passes through me as I experience a feeling of *déjà vu.*

Ten minutes ago, I drove the JEEP into the crushed oyster driveway and cut the engine. The cat and I exited the vehicle. Outside, the wind was blustery and the air humid, holding a fragrance of roses and cinnamon. The sun was an hour or so from setting, but swirling lavender clouds obscured the normal vibrant pink and orange sky, giving the atmosphere a slightly ominous vibe.

Now Callie and I are walking up the steps to the porch. I keep getting the shivers as my head swivels left and right. The dognapper's house is a small shotgun structure, painted peach with fuchsia trim. Dense clusters of unwieldy oleander trees are lined in rows on either side, planted to provide privacy. As the leaves sway back and forth, I can't help thinking how easy it would be for someone to hide among the branches.

I also can't help thinking that the cat and I have been in this situation before, and yet something feels different. More sinister, for some reason. A few months ago, Callie and I visited a house where we found a dead body. And then, a month later, we went to another house and discovered another dead body.

Walking toward the door, I'm getting the willies, and I'm thinking—

"Something's wrong, sis …" says the cat.

Jumping, I stop and glance down at her. "What do you mean?"

"The door is open," says Callie.

Shocked, I stare at the door.

The cat is right.

As I inch forward, I see a thin crack, a sliver of shrouded darkness between the door and the frame.

"Why would the door be open?" I ask.

"I don't think he forgot to close it," says Callie.

"Are you thinking what I'm thinking?" I glance down at the Calico.

She looks at me. "Well, are you thinking the dognapper is dead? Because that's what I'm thinking."

Panic threatens to explode within me, but I take a deep breath. "Why do you think he's dead?"

"Because I can sense it, sis," says the cat as she trots to the door. "I told you, cats know these things."

"Where are you going?" I ask, feeling spooked, glancing around me.

"I'm going inside."

"You think we should do that?" I ask, my voice a high-pitched squeak. "Maybe we should call the cops."

"You take care of that, sis," says the Calico, slipping her paw between the crack in the door.

"And what are you going to do?"

Pushing the door open wider, the fearless feline says, "I'm going to get the Corgi."

"The Corgi!" I shake my head, realizing I'd forgotten about the dog. Although, who could blame me? I've got a full case of the willies, considering my surroundings. The lavender clouds are growing thicker, and darker, shrouding what would be a glorious sunset. The oleander leaves rustle vigorously. Peering at them, I get the feeling someone is hiding in the bushes, waiting to pounce, but I know it's just the wind.

"The dognapper might be dead," says Callie. "But we still need to rescue the dog."

As Callie slips through the space in the door, and into the house, I take another quick look toward the oleander bushes.

"Hello?" I call out, feeling foolish. Why would someone be hiding in the bushes? And, if they are, would they answer me?

In response, the oleander leaves, flowered with vibrant pink petals, rustle, and shiver.

Taking a deep breath, I follow the cat into the house.

Chapter 33

The layout of the shotgun house is as I expected it would be.

The small living room is furnished sparsely, but it's tidy, with a divan, chair, and coffee table. A television is mounted on the wall. A long hallway leads to the galley kitchen on the left, bedrooms on the right, and a bathroom at the rear of the house.

Glancing around the living room, I see nothing that looks out of place. Moving to the kitchen, I spot a bag of dog food on the counter.

"Callie, did you see this?" I ask, glancing around for the cat. "At least the dognapper was feeding James Mortimer."

Makes sense, though. If he was going to get ransom money for the dog, he had to keep the poor canine alive and healthy.

"Girl, come take a look at this," calls out the Calico.

"Where are you?"

"Second bedroom."

Steeling myself for what I'm sure I'll find, I let out a shaky breath and walk the few steps across the narrow hallway, and toward the doorway of the second bedroom. I don't want to go into it. I don't want to find another dead body, but I can't be scared or squeamish. If I'm going, someday—hopefully soon—to be a top-notch investigative reporter, I have to get used to all the depraved and horrible things that go along with crime reporting.

Pushing past my hesitation, I step into the room.

Which is empty.

Well, not empty, exactly. There's a bed, a dresser, a bureau drawer, and bedside tables. Everything you'd find in a typical bedroom, but …

There's no dead body.

However, there is a faint, putrid smell of—

"The Corgi was here," says Callie, who's standing on the bed, looking over the side. "Come take a look …"

I walk to the opposite side of the bed.

On the floor is a small cage, inside of which are two bowls. One filled with water. The other with dry dog food. The cage is empty, the door open, and nearby is a puddle of what I suspect is canine urine.

"James Mortimer was here," I say. "But where is he now?"

"You search the house," says Callie. "I'll take a look outside. He might be hiding in the bushes."

As Callie leaps off the bed and trots out of the bedroom, I start to think she's right. That rustling in the Oleander leaves was probably the Corgi, frightened and confused.

Starting my search in the second bedroom, I look under the bed, and then in the closet. For good measure, I check the dresser and bureau drawers. How the Corgi could have gotten inside, I don't know. But, you never know. Anyway, not surprisingly, the dog is not in the second bedroom.

Leaving the bedroom, I check the bathroom. Clean and neat, nothing out of the ordinary.

I head toward the other bedroom, which is directly across from the kitchen.

Now I'm wondering if the dognapper grabbed the Corgi, and fled the house, leaving the door open, not bothering to make sure it was closed. After all, there was no car in the driveway. But why would the dognapper leave the house? He knew I was coming. He wanted the money. Did he get skittish about something? Maybe he worried that I would bring the police? Maybe the dognapper was in the bushes, watching me. That would make sense if he wanted to make sure I'd come alone.

Or maybe, I think, opening the closet door, the dognapper—

My thoughts flee as a scream bursts from my mouth.

A man is in the closet.

I don't know if he's the dognapper, but I do know this …

He's dead.

Red, sticky, blood stains the front of his yellow T-shirt.

"Oh, my God!" I gasp, backing away from the closet. "Callie! Callie!"

I turn from the ghastly scene and—

Something comes at me, as quick and fast as lightening.

Closing my eyes, I turn my head and hold up an arm, trying to block what I'm sure will be a blow, but I'm too late. A hard object crashes against the side of my face. Off balance, I stumble and fall to my knees. The hard object connects with the back of my head. I slump to the floor, confused and terrified, staring at the rug as darkness swallows me …

Chapter 34

"You do have a concussion," says Dr. Villalongo, his expression concerned.

Leaning back against the pillows, I glance at the plastic identification bracelet one of the nurses clamped around my wrist when I woke up in the hospital.

"I suspected you were going to say that," I say, glancing up at the doctor.

Things in my mind are foggy, but from what I was told, by the officers who were standing by my bedside to take my statement when I woke up, I was knocked out. Obviously. As for how I ended up in the back of an ambulance, they told me that the next-door neighbor alerted EMS, who arrived at the dognapper's house.

I was taken to the emergency room, evaluated, and treated. I woke up an hour or so later and was transferred from the ER to a hospital room, where I've been since yesterday.

"Because of the coma you were in a few months ago," says Dr. Villalongo, "I want you to stay another night in the hospital."

"Are you sure that's necessary?" I ask, wiggling my toes beneath the bed sheets. "I feel okay."

"Just because you feel okay, Ms. Sophia, doesn't mean that you are okay," the doctor says. "I don't mean to alarm you. I don't think anything is wrong, but you experienced a traumatic brain injury before so you need to be monitored."

"I know, I know," I tell him. "Just don't call my mom this time. She'll throttle me if she finds out about the concussion."

"As well she should," says Dr. Villalongo. "What on earth were you doing, Ms. Sophia, when you got conked in the head?"

Sheepish, I say, "I was trying to rescue Ms. Lux's missing Corgi. I'd gone to the dognapper's house to try to rescue the dog, but it didn't quite work out like that, and—"

"And it was too dangerous ..."

Excited, and chastened, by the familiar voice, I look toward the hospital door.

Dressed in uniform, Officer Cuetee walks into my room, and he's not alone ...

Nestled in his arms, snug, and content, is Callie. At first, I'm shocked that the Calico is so complacent, but I remember that Callie likes Officer Cuetee, and has allowed him to cuddle her.

"If not for this pretty girl," says Officer Cuetee, giving Callie a scratch behind her ear, eliciting a satisfied purr. "I wouldn't have known to tell the paramedics where to find you."

"Sorry ..." I say, biting my lip as the Calico jumps down onto the bed. "So, how did Callie ... get word to you that I was in trouble?"

"Girl, I totally saved the day," says the cat, stretching out at the foot of the bed. "You owe me, sis."

"The same way she did that other time when you were in trouble," says Officer Cuetee.

"I was outside looking for the Corgi," starts Callie.

"Did you find him?" I asked, immediately worried about the missing dog.

"Did I find who?" asks Officer Cuetee.

Kicking myself for talking to the cat when I'm talking to humans, something I'm not supposed to do, I clear my throat. "Um ... the dead guy in the closet?"

Licking her fur, the cat says, "Couldn't find him anywhere."

"Paramedics found him," says Officer Cuetee.

"That's a shame," I say, wondering what on earth could have happened to Ms. Lux's dog. Was he dognapped again? Possibly by the person who killed the guy I found in the closet? Or–

"It's a shame that the EMS guys found the dead body?" asks Officer Cuetee.

"Oh, um, no, of course not ..." I glance away from Officer Cuetee's perplexed expression. "I meant, it's a shame he was killed. Do you have any idea who murdered him?"

"Not yet," says Officer Cuetee. "We identified him as Novak Penegar. He was stabbed to death."

"So terrible," says Dr. Villalongo. "What is this island coming to?"

"Who killed the dognapper?" asks Callie.

"Cops don't know yet," I tell her.

"The police don't know what the island is coming to?" asks the doctor, his expression confused.

Again, I kick myself. "No, I meant—"

"Girl, I didn't finish telling you my story," says the cat, rising to all fours. "What was the last thing I said?"

Staring at Officer Cuetee, I say, "You were telling me how Callie saved the day?"

"Oh, yeah, that's right," says the cat. "So, I was outside looking everywhere for the Corgi, but I couldn't find him. So, I went back into the house to tell you I didn't have any luck, and there you were, sprawled out on the ground, knocked out cold. Naturally, I tried to wake you up, but you weren't moving. Girl, I knew I had to do something, so I went back outside and ran next door. I started scratching on the neighbor's door and meowing like I'd had too much catnip. The neighbor opened the door, and I kept meowing and jumping up toward the neighbor and trying to get the old coot to follow me, which he did, over to the dognapper's house. I kept meowing and he followed me into the bedroom where you were. Then he called an ambulance."

"Well, it was the craziest thing," says Officer Cuetee. "Dutiful and I were getting into the squad car when a dispatch sent us on a call—dead body in the Double H neighborhood. So, my partner and I drove over. We met the next-door neighbor outside who told us a cat was meowing and howling outside his door. When he stepped out onto the porch, the cat ran over to Novak Penegar's house. The neighbor had experience with cats and had a feeling the cat was leading him toward something. He thought he'd find a litter of kittens. Instead, you were unconscious on the floor and Penegar was dead in the closet. If not for the cat that's not your cat ..."

"She really did save the day," I say, giving the cat a smile.

"Girl, what else was I supposed to do?" asks the cat, giving me a look. "You are my human."

Blinking back tears, I nod.

I am Callie's human.

But, I'm not her real owner.

At once, I'm reminded of the strange, harrowing story told to me by Ms. Fong, from the St. Felipe Furry Friends Animal Shelter. Callie was abandoned in the middle of the night by someone driving the car of a dead man. The person who owned her gave her up. But why? Did her real owner not want her anymore? Or maybe wasn't able to take care of her?

I'm not sure, but I have to find out.

I want to keep Callie in my life, all to myself, but if she belongs to someone else, then—

"Sophie ..." says Officer Cuetee.

"Are you feeling okay, Ms. Sophia?" asks Dr. Villalongo.

"Girl, what's the matter with you?" demands the feline. "Is it your head? You're not going into the coma again, are you?"

Shaking my head, I say, "No …"

"You're not feeling well?" Dr. Villalongo rushes to my side.

"Oh, no, no …" I say, upset that I've worried the doctor and Officer Cuetee. "No, I'm feeling fine."

"But when I asked if you were feeling okay, you said no," says the doctor, giving me a skeptical gaze.

"I know, but I didn't mean that," I say. "I meant to say I was feeling fine. Because I am. Feeling just great."

Stroking his chin, the doctor says, "You may have had too much excitement. Officer, do you mind taking the cat so I can examine Ms. Sophia?"

Picking up the cat, Officer Cuetee says, "No problem."

"I don't want to leave, sis," says Callie. "I want to make sure you're okay."

"It's fine," I say, waving at Callie. "I'll be fine."

"I got you, girl," says Officer Cuetee, cradling the cat in the crook of his arm. "Sophie's going to be okay. We'll be back tomorrow. Let's go get you some kibble."

"Callie doesn't like kibble," I call out as Officer Cuetee heads out of the door.

"Girl, I don't like kibble from weird ladies who smile too hard and talk in sing-song," says the cat. "But, Officer Good Looking can give me kibble any time he wants!"

Chapter 35

"First of all, how are you doing?" asks Officer Cuetee.

"Doing great!" I say, taking a sip of tea. "Dr. Villalongo gave me the all-clear. No problems with my noggin."

Officer Cuetee and I are having Sunday afternoon tea at the Hibiscus Hotel, one of the swankiest, most expensive, ultra-exclusive hotels in St. Mateo. It's super fancy, which is an understatement, and the clientele is comprised of the crème de la crème of St. Mateo's upper-crust society, as well as famous athletes, celebrities, and politicians.

"That's good," says Officer Cuetee. "When I heard about your concussion, I was really worried."

"So was Callie," I say, spreading a delightful guava jam on a piece of croissant. "She keeps thinking I'm going to go back into the coma."

"Wait. What? The cat thinks you're going to go back into the coma?"

Staring at Noah's confused expression, I shove the croissant in my mouth, signaling that I'm eating and don't want to talk with my mouth full. Truth is, I need to stall for time. Another thing I have to remember not to do is talk about Callie like she's a human friend.

Swallowing, I grab my glass of water and take a long gulp. Placing the glass back on the table, I clear my throat, smile, and say, "So ... you wanted to tell me the new developments in the Novak Penegar murder case?"

Officer Cuetee gives me a dubious glance, and a little smirk that lets me know he's aware I avoided the subject of the cat, but he doesn't press the issue.

After all, he called me yesterday to inform me of interesting developments concerning the death of Novak Penegar, which is our official reason for meeting.

"Well, we determined that Penegar was stabbed with a Swiss Army knife."

"A Swiss Army knife?" I ask. "Wait. Wasn't Annie Stone killed with a Swiss Army knife?"

"Yes, she was," says Officer Cuetee.

"So do the police think that Novak Penegar and Annie Stone were killed with the same weapon?"

"Certainly looks that way."

I take another sip of tea. "But, that's really weird. Why would they be killed by the same person? I mean, why would the same person want both of them dead?"

"That's what Detective François is trying to figure out," says Officer Cuetee. "Right now, he's investigating the connection between Annie Stone and Novak Penegar."

"What connection between Annie Stone and Novak Penegar?" I ask.

"It's another interesting development," says Officer Cuetee. "The forensic IT department recovered Novak Penegar's cell phone and computer. Turns out, Novak and Annie exchanged hundreds of text messages and emails."

"They knew each other," I say.

"They more than knew each other," he says. "They were in cahoots with each other."

"In cahoots with each other?" I stare at Officer Cuetee. "I don't understand."

Officer Cuetee says, "Novak and Annie conspired to dognap James Mortimer."

"Are you serious?"

He nods. "The text messages prove it. Basically, Annie convinced Novak to help her steal the Corgi."

"What?" To say I'm shocked is an understatement. "But why?"

"Again, according to the emails and texts," says Officer Cuetee. "Annie was disgruntled and upset with Ms. Lux because she wouldn't give Annie a part in her new movie."

Nodding, I say, "That's why Annie was blackmailing Lucretia Lux. But, why would Annie ask for ransom money to return the Corgi? All she had to do was extort money from Lucretia."

"Well, there's an interesting development with that," says Officer Cuetee. "Detective François was able to get texts from Annie Stone's cell phone. She told Novak Penegar that Ms. Lux had tricked her."

"Tricked her?"

"Annie Stone lost her advantage over Lucretia Lux," says Officer Cuetee. "Ms. Lux told Annie she would give her a part in the movie but only if Annie gave Ms. Lux the video of Ms. Lux kicking the Corgi, which Annie did. But, then, not surprisingly, Ms. Lux rescinded the offer."

"That is interesting," I say. "And it means that Lucretia Lux didn't really have a reason to kill Annie Stone since Annie didn't have the surveillance video to blackmail Lucretia."

"I think that's what Ms. Lux told Detective François when he questioned her about slapping and threatening to kill Annie Stone," says Officer Cuetee. "Ms. Lux doesn't have a motive for murder, after all."

Frowning, I say, "But I heard her tell Esteban not to cross her and that she would get rid of him like she got rid of Annie Stone."

Officer Cuetee shakes his head. "Don't really know what to make of that. Anyway, Annie wanted to take the ransom money and start a new life somewhere. She planned to share the cash with Novak."

"Oh my goodness," I say, grabbing another croissant and slathering passionfruit butter across it. "So, wait. If Annie and Novak were working together, how did they end up dead?"

"Yeah, that's the question," says Officer Cuetee. "From the emails and texts, we were able to piece together how the dognapping would go. Annie always took James Mortimer to the dog park at night. While there, Novak would show up and Annie would give him the dog. Then Annie was going to call Ms. Lux, panicked, and crying, and tell her that while she was with James Mortimer at the dog park, someone pulled a gun on her and demanded the dog."

"But things didn't work out that way," I say. "Annie was killed at the dog park. And James Mortimer was dognapped. You think Novak is the killer?"

"It's possible," allows Officer Cuetee. "Annie and Novak might have had some sort of falling out that night at the dog park. And then Novak killed her."

"And took James Mortimer to ransom him and keep all of the money for himself," I say.

"But then who killed Novak Penegar?"

"Maybe he was working with someone," I say. "He might have teamed up with a partner that Annie didn't know about. And Novak could have had a falling out with his partner, who killed him."

"But remember Novak and Annie were killed with the same weapon," says Officer Cuetee. "The Swiss Army knife."

"So, that takes us back to someone who wanted both of them dead," I say. "But who could that be?"

Chapter 36

"I can't imagine who would want Annie Stone and Novak Penegar dead," I say, taking a sip of tea as I glance at Clark, sitting across from me.

We're taking our first break on a bleak Monday morning that's cloudy and gray. Outside, the weather looks nothing like paradise. No blue skies and bright sunshine for the tourists today, unfortunately.

"What about Ms. Lux?" asks Clark.

I shake my head. "I don't think so."

Clark takes a sip of coffee. "Why not?"

"Ms. Lux doesn't have a motive for killing Annie, after all, remember?" I say. "Officer Cuetee told me that she tricked Annie into giving her the dog-kicking video."

Clark removes his glasses to clean them with a small cloth he pulls from the pocket of his jeans. "True, but what if Ms. Lux was worried about copies of the dog-kicking video and she killed Annie Stone, just in case, you know?"

"Killed Annie just in case?" I ask, skeptical.

"Or, what if, somehow, Ms. Lux learned that Annie and Novak plotted to dognap James Mortimer? In her enraged grief, she stabbed

Annie," says Clark, putting his glasses back on. "And then, she learned where Novak was hiding and killed him."

"I suppose it's possible," I say, though I'm not quite on board with Clark's theory. "But …"

"But?"

"But you really think Ms. Lux would kill Annie and Novak because they kidnapped James Mortimer?" I ask. "Seems like an overreaction to me."

"People get homicidal over their animals," says Clark. "Ms. Lux could have been so outraged at the thought of Annie and Novak stealing the dog that she overreacted."

"Maybe …" I say, stirring my tea. "I just wish …"

"What?"

Glancing at Clark, I say, "I wish I could understand shorthand."

Giving me a little sympathetic smile, Clark says, "I wish I could get a message to my mom. The reception is terrible. It's kind of worrying."

I return his smile. "Oh, I'm sure they're okay. And I thank you for trying."

"You thank Clark for trying what?" asks Candace, strolling into the breakroom with her customary jaunty stride. "The hypnotist I told you about? Or the tentacle reader down at the beach?"

I give Clark a look, which he returns, adding an eye roll.

"No, Clark didn't try either of those things," I say.

"Well, you should have tried both," says Candace, opening the refrigerator. "Especially, the hypnotist."

"Why especially the hypnotist?" I ask.

Candace removes a bottle of water, then closes the fridge, and walks to the table. "She could have helped you figure out if you had repressed any memories."

"Repressed memories about what?" asks Clark.

"I don't have any repressed memories," I tell Candace.

Unscrewing the cap from her bottle of water, she takes a quick drink, then gives me a dubious look. "How do you know that you don't have any repressed memories if you can't remember the memories? That's why they're called repressed memories. Because you don't know that you have them. Because they're repressed."

Again, I give Clark a look, which he returns, but this time without the eye roll.

Clearing my throat, I say, "What Clark tried to do was call his mom to ask her about reading shorthand."

Candance frowns. "Reading shorthand?"

I tell Candace about Annie Stone's secret diary, written in shorthand, which I can't read.

"Interesting," Candace says. "Me and your mother have something in common."

"What do you mean?" asks Clark.

"I know how to read shorthand," announces Candace. "Where's the diary? I'll read it for you."

Chapter 37

"He is still stalking me," I read, staring at the words on the legal pad.

Words I wrote down as Candace deciphered Annie Stone's shorthand, revealing a disturbing narrative that still gives me the willies.

"So Annie had a stalker," says Callie, stretched out on the end of the chaise on my patio.

"Apparently," I say.

"Interesting," declares the feline. "Keep going."

Currently, I'm reading the secrets of Annie's diary to Callie, who showed up half an hour ago, when I was on the patio, drinking tea and ruminating on the diary's revelations.

Clearing my throat, I continue: *"I have told him time and again that I want nothing to do with him but he insists that we belong together …"*

"When did she write that?" asks Callie.

"A month ago," I say.

"Which means she was being stalked here on the island," the cat says.

Nodding, I say, "Which means her stalker could be the killer."

"Does she say that in the diary?" Callie asks.

"Unfortunately, no," I say.

"Does she name the stalker?"

"Regretfully, no," I say.

"Well, what else does she say?" demands the cat.

I glance at the legal pad. "Okay, she said ... *He keeps calling me ... and it seems like everywhere I go, he's there begging for a chance to be with me, telling me that he loves me and he can make me happy, but I don't want to be with him ... I can't get away from him. A few weeks ago, he tried to kiss me ... I slapped him ... and then he grabbed me and told me that if I didn't stop rejecting him, he would make my life miserable.*"

"Does she say how he was going to make her miserable?" asks Callie.

"No, but she does say that he sent her some disturbing texts," I say.

"Can you find the texts?"

"Well, the police have Annie Stone's cell phone," I say. "I could tell Officer Cuetee about the texts and he could tell the forensic IT department to look for texts between Annie and someone who might have been threatening her. Might be worth a shot. The cops might be able to trace those disturbing texts—that is, if they find them."

"Well, sis, we might not need the texts," says the cat.

"What do you mean?"

Callie says, "I know where the Corgi is ..."

Chapter 38

"Next time, lead with the bombshell revelation," I tell Callie as I turn into the parking lot of the Royal Azure, a small but exclusive luxury boutique hotel. Located in the island's interior, surrounded by lush rainforest, the hotel caters to wealthy tourists eager to take advantage of its beautiful location—and the hotel's liberal canine policy.

The cat stops licking her fur to stare at me. "What do you mean?"

"I mean," I say, circling the small lot, looking for a spot to park. "The first thing out of your mouth should have been that you'd found James Mortimer."

"Well, I didn't find James Mortimer, so I couldn't say that," counters Callie. "I said I know where he is …"

Sighing, I say, "You know what I mean. Your knowledge of the Corgi's whereabouts was much more important than Annie's diary, which really didn't tell us much."

"Speak for yourself, sis," says Callie. "I wanted to know what she wrote in that diary. And it did yield important clues. Now you know that you need to tell Officer Good-looking to look for those disturbing texts."

"True, but …" I say, pulling into an empty parking space.

"But we're here now, girl," says the cat, licking her fur again.

Conceding the point, I cut the ignition. "Okay, tell me again where James Mortimer is …"

"I heard he's hanging out with a Pomeranian who belongs to a security guard," says the cat. "They spend most of their time hiding out in the golf shop that's been closed for renovations."

After grabbing a hotel map from the lobby, which was busy so it was easy to slip past the clerks checking in guests, Callie and I pretended to be hotel patrons. With confidence I didn't actually have, I nevertheless followed the cat's lead, assuming the air of someone who belonged at the establishment.

After a long and winding jaunt across the hotel property, Callie and I approach the golf shop, festooned with yellow caution tape with a CLOSED sign in the window.

"Well, here we are, sis," says the cat, slinking around the side of the shop to the back. "Supposedly, the door is open."

Glancing at a utility door near the A/C unit, I look down at the feline. "Supposedly?"

"Well, according to my intel," says Callie, "the security guard allows the Pomeranian to hang out in the golf store while he's on duty."

"Speaking of your intel," I say. "Who told you where the Corgi was?"

"You got your anonymous sources, sis, and I got mine," says the cat. "Trust me. My info is legit."

Taking a deep breath, and an even bigger leap of faith in the cat, I walk to the door. Grabbing the knob, I twist it and push. The door opens.

"See?" says the cat, slipping inside the golf shop. "What did I tell you?"

I enter the shop. Inside, we're greeted with a dim, gloomy, and dusty renovation site. Guided by the fading sunlight streaming through the windows, I make my way carefully around ladders, paint cans, and buckets of joint compound. Abandoned drills, hammers, hard hats, and gloves litter a wooden sawhorse.

"Over here, girl," says the cat, disappearing behind a table covered with a paint-splattered cloth.

I follow the Calico.

Seconds later, glancing behind the table, I spot a fluffy little, orange-colored dog with a face that reminds me of a fox. The Pomeranian, I presume. The dog barks at Callie. The feline hisses at the dog.

"What's going on?" I ask, concerned about the confrontational nature of their exchange.

"Rainy—that's the Pomeranian's name—is just asking me how I knew she was here," says Callie.

"What did you say?"

The Pomeranian barks again.

Callie hisses again, then glances up at me. "I told her it doesn't matter. We didn't come here to talk to her. We want to talk to James Mortimer."

The Pomeranian advances toward Callie, her barking turning to a growl.

"Girl, she's trying to claim that the Corgi isn't here, but I smell the dog," Callie tells me, then advances towards the Pomeranian, hissing again.

"Is she going to let us talk to him?"

Callie says, "Girl, it's not up to her. Jimmy … come out here. Now! We don't have all day."

Worried, I tell the cat, "Don't scare him off."

But, the cat's fierce approach works.

Several sharp barks precede the sudden appearance of a haughty little canine with a long, low body and a distinctive regal bearing.

"James Mortimer," I say, recognizing the dog from the photo Esteban emailed me.

The dog stares at me, an imperial look with hints of scorn.

"Boy, you hear my human talking to you," says Callie, walking toward the dog.

The Pomeranian barks.

"Girl, whatever," says Callie to the Pomeranian. "This is not about you."

The Pomeranian lets forth several barking growls. Callie responds with guttural hisses, arching her back as she swats at the fluffy orange spitfire.

"Callie, can you please not fight with Rainy right now?" I implore. "We need to talk to James Mortimer."

For the next few minutes, Callie and Rainy bark and hiss. Every now and then, James Mortimer chimes in with an imperious bark, but mostly, he stands back, seemingly content to let the Pomeranian be his ambassador, which is not all that surprising. After all, technically, he's British royalty. And his human is an A-list actress who puts him on a pedestal. It's no wonder that he would allow another canine to do his bidding.

Finally, the cat and the Pomeranian settle down, and Callie walks over to James Mortimer.

"So, Jimmy, long time, no see," says the cat. "Where have you been all this time? People have been looking for you!"

"Tell him that his human has been worried sick," I say to Callie.

The Corgi barks.

"Girl, he said his human wasn't too worried about him," says the cat.

"Wait. Did the Corgi understand what I said?" I ask, slightly confused.

"All animals can understand humans, sis," says the cat, glancing back at me. "I told you that, remember. They just can't communicate with humans."

"But you can't understand any other human except me," I say.

"Right. But I don't know why, and it's not important right now," Callie says.

James Mortimer barks again.

"Girl, he says that if his human was really worried sick, she would have been looking for him day and night," translates Callie. "He says she wouldn't have eaten or slept until she found him. She would have made it her life's mission to bring him home."

"Interesting …" I comment, biting my lip, not surprised by the Corgi's narcissistic attitude.

"So, give us the tea, Jimmy," demands Callie. "And don't leave anything out."

The Pomeranian barks.

Callie hisses at Rainy. "Girl, if you don't stop—"

"Please, Callie," I say. "Focus on James Mortimer."

Callie says, "Fine. Fine. The tea, Jimmy. Spill it. Now."

The Corgi barks for a few minutes.

Callie says to me, "He says that the night he was dognapped, the actress's assistant—"

"Annie Stone," I supply.

"Right," says the cat. "Anyway, the assistant took him to the dog park, as she usually did so he could do his business and run around. And that's what he was doing, running around the park, when he noticed that Annie was talking to someone, a guy he'd never seen before. So Jimmy ran over—"

The Pomeranian emits a sharp couple of barks.

Callie glares at her. "Girl, I'll call him Jimmy if I want to. If he doesn't mind, then—"

"Focus, Callie," I remind the cat.

"Alright," says the cat. "But this would go a lot quicker and easier if Rainy would mind her business—"

"Callie!" I admonish.

"Calm down, sis," the cat tells me. "Anyway, Jimmy ran over when he saw Annie talking to the mystery guy."

"What were they talking about?" I ask.

"Girl, you are not going to believe it," says Callie. "Annie and the guy were discussing Jimmy's dognapping."

"Poor James Mortimer," I exclaim. "He knew they were going to dognap him. Why didn't he run away?"

Callie relays my question to the Corgi, who responds with a few barks.

"Girl, once again, you are not going to believe this," says Callie. "Jimmy didn't care that they were going to dognap him."

"Wait. What?"

"Girl, he claims he needed an adventure," the cat tells me. "He needed some time away from his human."

Flabbergasted, I say, "Time away from his human ..."

The Corgi barks again.

Callie says, "He says the actress is too needy. Too clingy. He wishes she would find a husband and leave him be."

"Well, maybe she will, " I say.

"Anyway, he was there when the assistant got stabbed," says Callie.

Flummoxed, I stare at the Corgi. "That must have been horribly traumatic for him."

The Corgi barks a bit more, and Callie says, "So, according to Jimmy, the assistant, Annie, picked him up and gave him to her friend."

"Novak Penegar," I say.

Callie says, "So, the friend tells Annie that he'll take Jimmy back to his place. And Annie will call the actress and tell her that she was attacked and some fiend—"

"A fiend?"

"Girl, the dog's word, not mine," says Callie. "Anyway, Jimmy and the friend headed out of the dog park. They were walking down one of the paths when the friend cursed and mumbled something about not having any money for dog food. So the friend turned and headed back to the dog park."

The Corgi barks at length.

When he finally stops, Callie says, "Jimmy says the friend got lost and they ended up on the opposite side of the dog park, he's not sure. All he knows is that they could see the dog park through some trees. The assistant was talking to another man."

"Another man?" I ask, riveted by the tale.

"Jimmy said the guy grabbed Annie and said something like, if I can't have you then nobody can have you," says Callie. "And then the assistant tried to get away but the man pulled out a knife and stabbed her. Over and over and over."

"Ohmigoodness …" I say, rubbing my arms, suddenly aware that the sun has set. The golf shop is even more gloomy. If not for the bright flood lights from the nearby golf course, it would be completely dark. Still, the illumination through the windows is faint and offers more shifting shadows than light.

I feel a case of the willies creeping upon me, but I've got to find out everything the Corgi knows before I take him back to Lucretia Lux. Once James Mortimer is home, safe and sound, I'm sure Ms. Lux won't let him out of her sight.

The Corgi barks once more.

Callie says, "And at that point, James Mortimer barked. The killer heard him, turned, saw the friend, and came after him. But the friend outran the killer and got away."

"Thank goodness!" I exclaim. "But it's too bad James Mortimer didn't bark before the killer stabbed Annie Stone. He might have startled the killer and scared him off."

"Girl, that's a good point," the cat tells me, then says to the Corgi, "Why didn't you stop the killer from stabbing the assistant?"

The Pomeranian, who'd been quiet, perks up with a series of sharp barks at Callie.

"Girl, nobody is blaming the victim, okay," says Callie to the Pomeranian. "But, really, Jimmy … what kind of guard dog are you?"

The Corgi barks vehemently, so aggressively that I take a step back.

"Yeah, I get it," says Callie. "You're not a guard dog. Obviously."

The Pomeranian yips a few times.

"Girl, she doesn't appreciate my sarcasm," Callie says.

"Well, sarcasm can be offensive," I say.

The Corgi barks once more, with slightly less vehemence.

Callie says, "Jimmy says he barked because the friend gripped him too tightly when they saw the assistant get stabbed. And furthermore, though he knows the killer's identity—"

"He does?" I ask, a jolt of excitement coursing through me. Finding Lucretia Lux's missing dog is already great for my career but I will definitely get booked on one of the major morning shows if I expose Annie Stone's killer.

The Corgi barks.

Callie says, "Jimmy says the same guy who killed Annie also killed the friend, Novak Penegar. He says the friend had let him out in the backyard to do his business. When he came back into the house, he heard the friend and the killer arguing about money."

"About money?"

Callie bobs her head. "And then the killer stabbed the friend, and

Jimmy got out of Dodge. Somehow, he made his way to the Royal Azure, hooked up with Rainy, and he's been here chilling since then, waiting for Ms. Lux to catch a clue and find him."

"Okay, so, who killed Annie Stone and Novak Penegar?"

"Don't get excited, girl," warns the cat. "Jimmy refuses to reveal the murderer."

"He refuses to reveal the murderer?" I'm stunned. "What? Why?"

"Jimmy thinks the assistant got what she deserved," says Callie. "He claims she was unkind and did not properly defer to him as she should have."

Exhaling, I say, "You're kidding."

"Jimmy said the man who killed the assistant was kind to him," says Callie. "Jimmy doesn't want to see him in jail."

"But, he can't just let the murderer go free," I say.

The Corgi barks then turns from me and trots under the table.

Callie says, "Jimmy isn't snitching. He said, and I quote—I'm not a rat ..."

Chapter 39

"James Mortimer!"

Lucretia Lux's high-pitched screaming squeal—or, maybe it's a squealing scream—is in the soprano range, so loud and sudden that Callie, the Corgi, and I all jump. Considering how cool, calm, and collected Lucretia Lux has been throughout this whole ordeal, it's a bit shocking to see her so animated and high-pitched. But, I supposed it's to be expected. She was probably suppressing her emotions, hoping against hope that James Mortimer would be found. Now that he's back in her arms, she can express all the pent-up feelings she held at bay.

"Oh, my baby!" Ms. Lux yanks the Corgi from my arms, where he was nestled, at his insistence. "Oh, my sweet precious baby!"

For the next few minutes, Lucretia Lux cradles the dog, cooing endearments as she kisses him. In her clutches, the dog squirms and emits barking yelps—or maybe yelping barks.

Sitting next to my right foot, Callie says, "The dog is not here for all her hollering and smooching."

I stifle a giggle as Lucretia rocks the Corgi like a baby, and the dog yelps again.

"She's upsetting his stomach," says Callie. "She better stop or he's gonna hurl."

Alarmed, I grab Ms. Lux's arm, stopping her movement. "So, Ms. Lux …"

Glaring at me, she says, "I hope you don't expect a reward."

"A reward?"

"There isn't one," she tells me.

"No, I don't want a reward, I just want—"

"You're not getting the ransom money, either," she says, snuggling the dog closer to her. "No, she's not, little one. She's not getting one dime!"

"Why would I want the ransom money," I say. "I didn't kidnap the dog."

Giving me a dubious glare, she says, "No, you didn't kidnap him. You did something even worse."

I'm confused. "Something worse?"

"You caused Detective François to suspect me of murdering Annie Stone!" Lucretia scowls at me. "Because of you, I could have been arrested. I could have been thrown in some third-world island prison and might have never seen my precious James Mortimer again."

"Oh … " I say, recalling the information about Lucretia slapping and threatening Annie Stone that I shared with Officer Cuetee, who passed the lead to François. "Well, you see … when I found out you had slapped and threatened Annie, I thought—"

"That I murdered her, too?"

Shrugging, I say, "You did sort of have a motive to kill her. Or, so I thought at the time. Before I found out that you tricked Annie Stone into giving you the dog-kicking video back, which meant you didn't have to kill her."

"Even if I hadn't gotten the video back," says Lucretia, turning to walk into the spacious foyer. "I wouldn't have killed Annie. I'm not a murderer."

Nodding, I say, following her. "But you did threaten to kill her."

"I didn't mean to do that. I shouldn't have done it," says Ms. Lux, gliding into the living room. "I said something horrible in the stress of a moment when I was panicked. Annie was being ridiculous, mean-spirited, and unreasonable. I never wanted her to die, even though she was blackmailing me, which is what I explained to the detective."

"I'll catch up with you later, sis," says Callie.

Glancing down at her, I ask, "Where are you going?"

"To talk to Klaus," she says. "He'll probably want to know what happened to Annie. They were close, remember?"

The cat trots away, hurrying down a long hallway off the living room while I join Ms. Lux, taking a seat on the couch across from the couch where she perches, legs tucked beneath her, cradling James Mortimer.

"So, you threatened Annie to scare her?"

The actress plants more kisses on James Mortimer's head, then looks up at me. "I didn't want to scare her. I said I would kill her in the heat of the moment. What I really wanted was for her to stop insisting that I give her a part in my movie. She wasn't an actress. I was more than happy to pay her handsomely for the video, but she refused."

Clearing my throat, I say, "Listen, I have to be honest with you. I overheard you telling Esteban that you would get rid of him like you got rid of Annie if he crossed you. So, that's really why I thought you'd killed her." ."

She shakes her head. "When did you hear me say that?"

"When you and Esteban came to the *Palmchat Gazette* to meet with me, Marty, and Detective François about the ransom sting operation," I say. "After the detective left—"

"I meant I would fire him like I fired Annie," she says, lips pursed in irritation.

"You would fire him?" I ask, perplexed. "Wait. You fired Annie?"

Lucretia says, "I told her that once I left the island, which I plan to do next month, I would no longer need her services. And because I try to be a decent employer, I informed her that she could continue to work for me, if she wished, up until that time."

"And you threatened to fire Esteban because …?"

"Because I thought, at the time, that he'd told the detective I slapped and threatened Annie," she says. "But, I recently learned, from Detective François, that you were responsible for that bit of information. So, tell me, how on earth did you find out?"

"Well …" I hesitate, knowing I can't tell Lucretia I got the clue from a turtle, then say, "I think Chef Bonnie told me."

Lucretia rolls her eyes. "Figures. I never trusted her."

Eager to change the subject, I say, "Ms. Lux, did Detective François tell you Annie Stone conspired with a man named Novak Penegar to steal James Mortimer?"

"He did. And, I supposed I'm not surprised," she says, peppering the Corgi with a barrage of kisses as he squirms and yelps, probably for dear life. "Annie obviously wanted to get back at me for thwarting her extortion attempts. François asked me if I knew Novak Penegar, but I've never heard of the man. I know nothing about his connection to Annie. I know nothing about who killed Annie or Novak Penegar."

"No idea, at all?" I ask. "No suspicions of anyone?"

Shaking her head, Lucretia says, "I thought it was Bonnie, but I was wrong about that. All I know is that I didn't kill Annie. Not only did I take a lie detector test, which I passed, but I have an alibi."

I bite my lip, then say, "So, Annie wasn't killed by you, Bonnie, or her dognapping partner in crime, Novak Penegar, so, maybe Annie's stalker killed her."

Lucretia gives me a confused look. "Annie's stalker? What stalker? Annie was being stalked?"

"You didn't know about the stalker," I guess.

"I had no idea," she says. "How would I have known? She didn't tell me. And how did you know?"

"Anonymous source," I say quickly.

"Have you told the police about this stalker?" demands Lucretia.

"No, but—"

Yelping loudly, the Corgi squirms his body from Lucretia Lux's arms, leaps to the floor, and scampers away.

"Oh, James Mortimer! Darling, come back to mommy!" Lucretia Lux jumps up. "Oh, the poor dear! What those horrid dognappers must have put him through to make him so terrified and skittish. He must be suffering from horrible anxiety and PTSD. I might need to call a canine psychotherapist."

"A canine psychotherapist?"

Lucretia says, "A dog shrink. Please, you'll have to see yourself out. I need to find James Mortimer. Those annoying turtles from the lake keep finding their way into the house, despite Esteban's attempts to get rid of them, and I don't want my poor baby to get bitten!"

Chapter 40

"Ms. Lux was telling the truth about having an alibi," says Officer Cuetee when I reach him on the phone the next morning.

I called Noah after I enjoyed a cup of clementine tea and lime-glazed donut holes, which I felt I deserved. After all, I found James Mortimer, returned him to Ms. Lux, and wrote a quick story about the dog's return, which I emailed to Marty and which he didn't exactly love, but he nevertheless had the story uploaded to the paper's online website.

JAMES MORTIMER FOUND!! began to trend immediately. And while the story didn't exactly break the internet, it did go completely viral. Already, tons of newspapers and news outlets, and news stations have picked up the story. The Corgi's social media accounts have gone insane with likes, shares, and comments of gratitude for his safe return.

Additionally, my social media accounts have gained traction and followers. People are curious about me and want to know who I am, and more about me, which is nice. Unfortunately, I haven't been booked on any of the morning shows yet, but I'm not giving up hope.

"She was?" I ask, though I'm not surprised. I didn't think she lied to me, but it's good to have confirmation.

"Video surveillance proved she was telling the truth," says Officer Cuetee. "Lucretia Lux was video chatting with her agent during the time Annie Stone was being murdered."

"So, she has an alibi for Annie Stone's death," I confirm, making notes on a sticky pad. "But, what about Novak Penegar?"

"Again, she has an alibi," he says. "Ms. Lux was having dinner with friends. The medical examiner estimated Penegar's time of death at about an hour before you arrived at Penegar's house, around six p.m. Her driver, Esteban, confirmed that he dropped her off at the restaurant and picked her up four hours later, around ten later that night."

"Well, I guess that proves that Ms. Lux didn't knock me out," I say. "Whoever conked me over the head probably killed Novak Penegar and Annie Stone."

"Question is, who hit you?" asks Officer Cuetee.

"I have no idea," I say. "Do the police have any leads?"

"We're still processing the evidence," he says. "We collected a few prints and trace DNA, so hopefully, we'll get a match soon."

"Do you know if the cops found any threatening text messages on Annie Stone's phone that appeared stalkerish?" I ask.

"Stalkerish text messages?" asks Officer Cuetee.

"Annie Stone was getting disturbing text messages from a stalker."

"How do you know that?"

"She wrote about it in her diary," I say.

"Annie Stone had a diary?" asks Officer Cuetee.

"She did," I say. "Another anonymous source told me about it. Anyway, I read it, which I know is awful because you're not supposed to read another person's diary, but—"

"Does she identify the stalker in her diary?"

"Unfortunately, no," I say. "But I was thinking maybe the IT department could search her phone for the threatening messages."

"I'll let François know," says Officer Cuetee. "And he'll probably want to see the diary, too. You have it with you?"

"Actually, I do," I say, glancing at my INBOX, where I placed Annie Stone's diary after Candace translated it. "But, I have to warn you. It's written in shorthand."

"We have a few admins who know shorthand," he says. "I'll stop by in a few hours to pick it up."

After ending my conversation with Officer Cuetee, I lean back in my chair and glance up at the stained ceiling tiles. With Ms. Lux and Chef Bonnie cleared as suspects, that leaves Annie Stone's stalker as the person most likely to have killed her.

Based on what James Mortimer told Callie, I'm sure the stalker followed Annie to the dog park, then attacked her after she handed the Corgi off to Novak Penegar. When Novak returned to get money for dog food, he saw the stalker stab Annie, which made him a target.

If the stalker is the killer, then who is the stalker? And how can I find out?

I glance at the diary.

Could the stalker's identity be hidden in the shorthand? I'm not sure. Candace found and deciphered all of the passages that Annie Stone wrote about the stalker. Lucretia Lux's assistant didn't mention the stalker by name, but she may have, inadvertently, provided clues about who he is.

I lean forward and grab the diary, where I left my transcribed notes. Opening it, I flip toward the middle, and—

An envelope falls from the back of the diary and lands on my lap.

Confused, I pick it up and open it. Inside, is a note, which I remove, and read.

ANNIE,

I LOVE YOU AND I WILL NOT STOP. I KNOW YOU
LOVE ME, TOO, BUT FOR SOME REASON, YOU WILL NOT
ALLOW YOURSELF TO BE WITH ME. THE LOVE I HAVE
FOR YOU IS CLASSIC AND TIMELESS. I CAN GIVE YOU A
BETTER LIFE THAN THE ONE YOU HAVE. NEITHER OF
US HAS TO SPEND THE REST OF OUR DAYS DOING THE
BIDDING FOR PEOPLE WHO CARE NOTHING ABOUT US!
PLEASE ALLOW ME TO BE THE MAN YOU DESERVE.
STOP PUSHING ME AWAY.
WE WILL BE TOGETHER, NO MATTER WHAT, I
PROMISE YOU THAT.
I WANT TO LIVE WITH YOU BUT IF I CAN'T, THEN
WE WILL BE TOGETHER IN DEATH!

Shuddering, I read the note again, which is written in slanted block letters that look sort of important, or imperial, if that makes sense, although I'm sure it doesn't, but, anyway.

Obviously, it was written by the stalker. But, unfortunately, he didn't sign his name. I focus on the phrase, *we will be together in death*. Was that a death threat? Was the stalker telling Annie that he would kill her if she refused to be with him? I bite my lower lip, wondering. The stalker promised they would be together in death, which makes me think, if he planned to kill Annie, that he might have also planned to kill himself.

Exhaling, I place the note and the envelope on top of the diary.

Is it possible that the stalker is dead?

Thinking back to what James Mortimer told Callie, after Annie was stabbed, her attacker chased after Novak Penegar. So, could the stalker have killed himself after he tried to catch Novak? And if the stalker planned to commit a murder-suicide, then why would he bother chasing Novak? The stalker most likely went after Novak because he thought the dognapper had seen him kill Annie. And the stalker wanted to make sure Novak didn't tell the police.

Of course, the stalker couldn't have known that, instead of calling the cops to report Annie's murder, Novak decided to hold James Mortimer for ransom, proving that old adage—no honor among thieves. However, since it's likely that Annie and Novak were killed by the same person, then the stalker must have been stalking—pun intended—Novak, waiting for the best opportunity to kill him.

These speculations, though unfounded, lead me to believe the stalker probably isn't dead. He probably didn't mean to kill himself.

I want to live with you but if I can't, then we will be together in death!

Those words were written to frighten Annie into a relationship with him.

Hopefully, those threatening words will help the cops find out the identity of the stalker.

Chapter 41

"You know what just occurred to me," says Clark.

After a sip of tea, I ask, "What?"

"James Mortimer knows who killed Annie Stone and Novak Penegar," says Clark. "Not that he could tell us."

"True …" I say, even though it's not. Well, it's not exactly true. Or, that is, it's partly true. James Mortimer does know who killed Novak Penegar. And Annie Stone. But he can tell us. That is, he could tell Callie and she could tell me, but the Corgi refuses.

After all, as Callie said, James Mortimer told her, *I'm not a rat.*

"Well, I'm hoping the police can come up with the identity of the stalker from Annie Stone's diary," I say.

Two days ago, I gave the diary, and the threatening note most likely written by the stalker, to Officer Cuetee, who promised to give the items to Detective François.

"I wonder why Annie didn't write the name of her stalker," says Clark, shaking his head.

"I don't know, either," I agree. "But I wish she had. I'm almost certain that her stalker killed her. If she had identified him, we'd know who killed her."

"So," says Clark, taking a sip of his black coffee. "Does your boyfriend have any new updates?"

"My boyfriend?" I ask, frowning as I take another sip of tea.

Giving me a playful smirk, Clark says, "Officer Cuetee …"

Rolling my eyes, I say, "He's not my boyfriend."

"Does he know that?" asks Clark, his tone teasing.

Tempering my irritation, I say, "He's my confidential police source."

"If you say so," says Clark.

Exhaling my annoyance, I say, "Anyway … unfortunately, no, there are no updates. The cops are going to talk to Ms. Lux about the diary. Maybe they can shed some light on who Annie's stalker might be."

"Annie never went to the cops about her stalker?"

I shake my head. "Officer Cuetee says Annie never reported that she was being stalked. However, it's possible that she told one of the other staff members about the stalker."

Nodding, Clark says, "You should ask the chef. And maybe the driver, too."

"Good idea," I tell him, finishing my tea. "I think I'll start with the driver, Esteban."

Minutes later, back at my desk, I loop my cross-body purse over my head and then grab my keys. Outside in the parking lot, I walk toward my JEEP, keeping an eye out for Callie. The cat is known to appear without warning, and I frequently find her sitting on the hood of my car. More often than not, the feisty feline will accompany me on my adventures, providing sarcastic, but supportive commentary.

But, not today.

Which actually might be a good thing, I think as I climb into the vehicle, buckle up, and start the car. I'm heading to Ms. Lux's beach house to talk to Esteban, who has a notorious allergy to cats. He won't be able to answer my questions if he can't stop sneezing.

Thinking about talking to Esteban, I probably should make sure he's at the beach house.

I unzip my purse and delve my hand inside, fishing around for my smartphone. When I pull it out, there's something stuck on the screen. Frowning, I stare at the blush pink colored 5x7 sticky note. What is …?

At once, the memory returns.

"Can you give Ms. Carter the photo of James Mortimer and my contact information?"

Ms. Lux gave me her contact information when I met her for the first time at the dog park. Esteban wrote it down on the sticky note.

LUCRETIA L. LUX
2 GOLDEN GRAVEL WAY
ST. MATEO, PALMCHAT ISLANDS

A sly jolt passes through me as I stare at the words Esteban wrote.

Something about the words set off loud, clanging alarms.

No, it's not the words that terrify me. It's the writing. That is, it's how the words are written. It's the handwriting. Esteban's handwriting.

I've seen it before …

Closing my eyes, I call forth a mental picture of different words that the driver wrote.

Horrific, sinister words.

I WANT TO LIVE WITH YOU BUT IF I CAN'T, THEN WE WILL BE TOGETHER IN DEATH!

Chapter 42

"You want to set a trap to catch Esteban the driver?" asks Callie.

"Yes ..." I say, pacing around the chaise lounge, where the cat is stretched out, licking her fur, on my patio.

The sun is setting, leaving a sky streaked and striped with creamy oranges, pinks, and lavender, but I hardly notice the breathtaking beauty. I'm too busy trying to recover from the fact that Esteban, Ms. Lux's driver, is a stalker and a killer. A stalking killer. A killing stalker.

Earlier today, after I realized that Esteban's handwriting on the blush pink sticky note matched the note written by the stalker, I hurried back into the *Palmchat Gazette* to confer with Marty about my speculations. Unfortunately, my boss wasn't around. Candace told me he had meetings outside the office all day. So, I ran my theory by Clark.

"And you're sure the handwriting is the same?" asked Clark.

"I am absolutely positive," I told him.

"But you gave the diary to the cops," Clark reminded me. "So you don't have the threatening note to compare to the sticky."

"I don't need the threatening note," I said. "I know I'm right. I remember that handwriting because it was very distinctive. Very elitist and regal."

"Elitist and regal?"

"It's hard to explain," I said to Clark. "But, trust me. Esteban wrote the contact information on the sticky note and he wrote the threatening letter to Annie Stone. Esteban is Annie's stalker. He killed her and he killed Novak Penegar."

Clark said, "Then you need to tell the cops."

"Yeah, I will, but …"

"But … what?"

"But, I was planning to talk to Esteban, so—"

"Sophie, no," said Clark, apprehension in his gaze. "If Esteban is the murderer, then you can't confront him. It's too dangerous."

Callie glances at me. "I hope you listened to your good-looking coworker."

Sighing, I nod. "I didn't go and confront Esteban. Even though I wanted to …"

"So what is this nonsense about setting a trap?" asks the Calico.

Glancing at the cat as I make another pass around the lounge, I say, "It's like I just told you. Detective François never takes me seriously. He won't even take my calls. I'll have to leave a message on his voicemail. Who knows when he'll check it? If Esteban is going to be caught, then I have to do it …"

"Girl, if you don't stop acting like you don't have the sense God gave a nanny goat," warns Callie.

Holding up my hands, I say, "Look, I know my plan will be risky—"

"Wait, this trap you want to set …" The cat stands on all fours. "It's a sting operation, isn't it?"

"No, not exactly," I say. "I mean, technically, I don't think it's a sting. I think it would be considered setting a trap but—"

"Setting a trap. Pulling a sting operation. Doesn't matter, sis," says Callie. "You can't do it. Not only will it be dangerous but it won't work. Girl, when have you ever done a successful sting operation?"

"Look, I'm not good at sting operations," I say. "I'll admit that. But I might be better at setting traps. Callie, I have to try."

"Says who?" demands the cat. "Girl, you need to tell Officer Cuetee."

"Yeah, I guess you're right," I say, pausing my pacing to sit on the edge of the lounge.

"Girl, I know I am," says the feline, licking her fur.

Chuckling, I say, "Well, now that that's settled, I was thinking that after the sting operation, we need to get back on the search for your real owner."

Callie stops licking her fur and glares at me. "You really think so? Last time we looked for my owner, you went to the wrong house."

"I know, but I think that was done on purpose," I say.

"You went to the wrong house on purpose?"

"No, I meant, I think whoever had you microchipped gave a fake name and address on purpose."

"Are you sure?"

"That's the only thing that makes sense. Don't you think?"

The cat stretches out on the lounge, looking away from me.

"Anyway, recently, I got a lead about someone leaving you in the parking lot of an animal shelter," I say. "But the people at the shelter don't know who left you. And then one day …"

"And then one day … what?"

"The shelter says you … disappeared."

The cat turns her head to stare at me. "Disappeared? What does that mean? What happened to me? Where did I go? Did I escape? Did somebody take me?"

"I don't know," I admit, feeling helpless and hopeless. "I'm not sure. It doesn't make sense, but I'm going to figure out—"

"Don't worry about it, sis," says Callie.

"What? I don't understand—"

"You've told me what I need to know," the cat says, rising to all fours. "Obviously, I wasn't wanted so whoever owned me just abandoned me. As for why I disappeared, it doesn't matter."

Heartbroken for Callie, I say, "But it does matter. Your disappearance was very mysterious and I think—"

Hissing, Callie says, "Just leave it alone, sis! Don't bother!"

"But, Callie—"

Ignoring me, the cat leaps from the lounge to the balcony railing and then down to the ground, where she takes off across the wide lawn behind my apartment complex.

Chapter 43

"Sophie, you're no good at sting operations, you know that," says Officer Cuetee.

As soon as I got to work this morning, I called the police station, hoping to speak with him, but he was out, so I got some work done—revising articles, fact-checking, and following up with witnesses. Then I went to lunch and called the police station again, but he was still out on calls. I was beginning to think I would never reach him. But, I finally did, and was able to tell him about my idea to set a trap for Esteban, Lucretia Lux's driver, the heinous murderer who killed Annie Stone and Novak Penegar.

"Oh, you sound just like Callie," I grumble, though I feel a bit wistful … and slightly worried, remembering the cat's assessment of my ability to pull off a sting. Which was three days ago. I haven't seen Callie since she took off like she was being chased by a pack of wild dogs. We'd been talking about her mysterious disappearance, which upset her, and then she … disappeared.

I've tried not to wring my hands, but I'm super upset. I should have done a better job of breaking the terrible news to Callie about the mysteries surrounding her past. I should have known she would be hurt and disappointed. I hate to think of her alone somewhere, feeling sad and hopeless, and unwanted.

More than anything, I want Callie to be my cat. Not just a cat I know. She needs to know that I want her in my life and I would never abandon her in the parking lot of an animal shelter in the middle of the night.

And I will tell her those things.

If she ever comes back …

Officer Cuetee asks, "What? I sound just like Callie? You mean, the cat you know who's not your cat? That Callie?"

Mentally kicking myself for the slip, I say, "Okay, you're right. I'm bad at sting operations. But, this is setting a trap. So, technically, it's different."

"A sting is a trap," says Officer Cuetee.

"Okay, well …" I take a deep breath. "You know, I'm never going to get good at sting operations or setting traps if I don't keep trying to get better at doing sting operations and setting traps."

Exhaling, Officer Cuetee shakes his head at me, his handsome face a mix of annoyance and amusement.

"Do you agree?" I ask, leaning back in my chair, staring at the computer on my desk.

After a pause, Officer Cuetee says, "Actually …"

"Actually?" I prompt, hopeful.

"Detective François is not as excited about the handwriting angle as I thought he would be," admits Officer Cuetee.

"Why not?"

"Well, to be fair, Detective François doesn't really get excited about anything," he says. "But, he wants the two handwriting samples analyzed before he questions Esteban."

Shaking my head, I ask, "Why?"

"He wants the handwriting evidence to be airtight, if the samples are, in fact, a match," says Officer Cuetee. "François doesn't want to tip off Esteban. He wants to have evidence against him when he questions him. He doesn't want Esteban to know the police suspect him. He might disappear."

"True," I say. "But why did you say actually ..."

"Because I don't necessarily agree with Detective François," says Officer Cuetee. "I think Esteban should be questioned about Annie Stone's stalker. He doesn't have to be confronted. Not yet, anyway. We could just see what he has to say. He might come clean. Stranger things have happened. If we get him talking about Annie, he might inadvertently reveal his true feelings about her. He might slip up and incriminate himself."

"So ... you think I should set a trap for Esteban?"

"I didn't say that ..."

"Well, why don't you hear my idea first," I say. "And then you can decide."

"Okay, what's your idea?"

It takes about thirty minutes, give or take a few seconds, for me to fully explain my plan to set the trap that will catch Esteban in his vicious lies, and prove him as the killer of Annie Stone and Novak Penegar.

"Well ...?" I prompt.

Officer Cuetee says, "Well ... it's so crazy, it just might work."

Squealing my delight, I say, "I knew you would like it!"

"But, Sophie, if your plan does work," says Officer Cuetee, his tone grim and stern, "and Esteban agrees to meet with you, then I am coming with you."

Smiling, I say, "Absolutely!"

Chapter 44

Fifteen minutes after I hang up with Officer Cuetee, and with the aid of vanilla tea—which would go perfectly with coconut cinnamon donut holes, but alas, I don't have any—I pick up my desk phone and dial the number of Esteban.

My heart pounds and my pulse races as the line rings, but I'm not worried about being nervous. I don't expect to be cool, calm, and collected. After all, I am calling a murderer. And no, I don't have any proof that Esteban is a killer, other than the sticky note with his regal handwriting which matches the handwriting on the threatening letter I found in the back of Annie's diary. And, again, no, I have no scientific proof that the handwriting on the sticky notes is the same as the handwriting on the threatening letter, but—

"Hello …?"

My heart lurches, and I swallow my fear. Or, I try to … but, I end up coughing, and have to clear my throat.

"Hello …? Is someone there?"

"Yes, yes, I'm here," I say, clearing my throat again. "Pardon me. Sorry. Um, would you mind if I took a quick sip of tea?"

"Would you mind telling me who you are and why you're calling?"

"Oh. Yes. Right. Of course," I say. I grab my mug of tea, take a quick sip, then say, "Sorry. This is Sophie Carter, from the *Palmchat Gazette.*"

"Ms. Carter. How are you?"

"I'm doing well," I say. "How are you?"

"Doing well," says Esteban. "And very happy that you found Ms. Lux's dog. Things are much happier here now that James Mortimer is home and ... oh, man, not again ..."

"What is it?" I ask, picking up on the exasperation in his tone.

"These crazy turtles," says Esteban.

"Crazy turtles?" I ask, recalling the turtle whose clue led me to suspect that Lucretia Lux killed Annie Stone.

"They keep getting into the house," says Esteban. "I'm not sure how to get rid of them, but Ms. Lux wants them gone. Anyway, how can I help you?"

"Well, I'm glad you asked," I say, and truthfully, I am because I was wondering how I was going to segue into my plan to trap him.

"Why is that?"

"Because I called to help you."

"Help me?" Esteban sounds confused. "I don't understand."

I grab my mug and take another sip of tea for fortification, then say, "I'm going to help you stay out of jail."

Chapter 45

"And then what did Esteban say when you said that?" asks Clark, taking a sip of coffee.

"Well, of course, he didn't know what I was talking about," I say, recalling the conversation with Esteban, which I concluded twenty minutes ago. As soon as I hung up the phone, I buzzed Clark and asked him to meet me in the breakroom, where we currently are, sitting at a table next to the wall of glass windows.

"So I told him I have undeniable proof that he killed Annie Stone and Novak Penegar."

"And he said?"

"Again, he claimed not to know what I was talking about," I say. "And then he said I didn't know what I was talking about because he would never kill anyone. And then he continued to deny being a murderer. And finally, he demanded to know what proof I had, which further convinced me that he is the killer."

Nodding, Clark says, "An innocent person would continue to deny being a murderer and would keep telling you that you're wrong. They wouldn't care about the evidence you claim to have because it wouldn't matter to them."

"Exactly," I say, thrilled that Clark and I are on the same page in the same book. "A guilty person wants to know what evidence you have on them, so they can figure out how to refute it."

"Did you tell Esteban about his handwriting matching the handwriting on the threatening letter?"

"I did," I say. "And, at first, he denied writing the letter, but then I told him that Annie Stone identified him as her stalker in her diary. He told me that he didn't believe me and demanded that I show him the diary."

"But you don't have the diary," Clark says.

Nodding, I say, "But Esteban doesn't know that. He thinks that I'm going to give him the diary."

"Why would you give him the diary?" asks Clark, frowning.

"Esteban and I made a deal," I say. "I give him the diary and he gives Ms. Lux a copy of the script I wrote and gets her to read it and produce it as her next movie."

Clark gapes at me. "You wrote a script?"

"Of course, I didn't write a script," I say. "But Esteban doesn't know that."

"Okay, I'm confused," admits Clark. "How is this deal you made with Esteban going to trap him into confessing to his crimes?"

"Well, it's simple," I say. "I'm going to tell Esteban that if he wants the diary, he has to confess to murdering Annie Stone and Novak Penegar."

"And you think he's going to do that?"

I take a sip of tea and say, "He will if he wants the diary."

"What if he refuses to confess?" asks Clark. "What if he knocks you out and takes the diary? I mean, if he killed Novak Penegar, and like you, I believe he did, then he's hit you and knocked you unconscious before."

"Don't remind me," I say, shuddering at the memory.

"I think I need to," says Clark, concern in his gray-green eyes. "Esteban already killed two people. The guy is unhinged and homicidal. He probably agreed to the deal because, when the two of you meet, he plans to kill you."

"Well, he's not going to kill me," I say, feeling rather smug. "Because I won't be alone."

"Let me guess," says Clark. "You're taking that cat you know with you?"

The thought of Callie, the cat I know, bums me out for a few moments. "I wish I was, but ... I don't know where she is. I haven't seen her for a few days."

Shrugging, Clark says, "She'll probably come back around. Cats are like that. They need space."

"I hope you're right," I say. "Anyway ... Esteban is not going to kill me because Officer Cuetee is coming with me to meet him."

"Ah, Officer Cuetee ..."

"Do. Not. Smirk," I warn Clark.

Smirking, Clark says, "Am I smirking? Why would I smirk?"

Rolling my eyes, I say, "So ... Officer Cuetee and I will give Esteban the deal. If he wants the diary, he has to confess to the murders."

"And you really think Esteban is going to confess in front of a cop?"

"Officer Cuetee will be undercover, in plainclothes," I say. "And I'll tell Esteban his confession is insurance. I can't just hand over the diary without any assurance that he'll get Ms. Lux to produce my script."

"Basically, you'll be using his confession to blackmail him into helping you start a career as a screenwriter."

"Exactly!" I confirm.

Leaning back in his chair, Clark grabs his coffee and takes a sip.

"What do you think?"

"I think I'm glad that Officer Cuetee will be with you," admits Clark. "When are you meeting Esteban?"

"Tomorrow at three in the afternoon ..."

Chapter 46

"Where you headed, sis?"

"Callie!" My heart lifts and soars at the familiar, sassy voice and I spin around, exhilarated, and excited as the Calico trots toward me. "Oh, my goodness! Where have you been? I was so worried!"

Moments ago, I exited the *Palmchat Gazette* offices. Shielding my eyes from the bright sunshine, I strode toward my JEEP, nervous and thrilled, anxious to meet with Officer Cuetee and carry out my plan to trap Esteban, the stalker killer.

Licking her fur, the cat asks, "Worried about what?"

"You!" I say, resisting the urge to pick the cat up and hug her to my chest.

Callie gives me a look. "Why?"

Feeling sheepish, I say, "I was worried I might never see you again…"

Tilting her head to the side, Callie asks, "Why would you never see me again?"

I let out a sigh. "Well, you know … the last time we talked, you got mad at me because—"

"Oh, girl, I was just feeling some kind of way, but I'm over it."

"Well, that's good," I say, even though I don't believe her. But I'm not going to press the issue because I'm happy she's back. The last thing I want is to drive her away.

"So, sis, you going to answer me anytime soon?" asks the cat, looking up at me. "Where are you headed? You look like you're up to something."

"Well, you're probably not going to like this, but ..." I start, opening the driver's door.

"I'm probably not going to like what?" demands the cat as she jumps up into the JEEP. "What are you planning? Don't tell me you're going to do that ridiculous, risky sting operation?"

"Okay," I say, getting into the vehicle as Callie settles into the passenger's seat.

"Okay, what?"

"I won't tell you that I'm going to do the ridiculous, risky sting operation," I say, closing the door and starting the JEEP.

"So, you are going to do the sting operation?" asks the feline, licking her leg.

Staying silent, I check my rearview mirror and then back out of the parking space.

"Girl, did you hear me?" asks the feisty feline. "Or, are you going deaf?"

"You told me not to tell you—"

"Does Officer Good Looking know what you're planning?" demands Callie. "Because he's not going to be happy when he finds out—"

"For your information," I begin, a bit smugly, "Officer Cuetee not only knows about the sting operation, but he approves of it."

"You're kidding?"

"Well, okay, he doesn't really approve, but he doesn't disapprove," I say, driving toward the side street I'll take to get to the main boulevard that functions as the main artery through town. "And, he's going to help me with the sting."

"You're joking?" deadpans the cat. "Has he lost his mind, too?"

"The sting is going to work this time," I say, using my indicator to signal a left turn into the flow of traffic. "Nothing bad will happen because Officer Cuetee will be by my side."

"If you say so, sis," says the cat as she curls up onto the seat. "I still don't like the sting operation idea but since Officer Handsome will be with you, I don't have to worry. I can get some much-needed rest ..."

Chapter 47

"I'm sorry, Sophie," says Officer Cuetee. "I'm not going to be able to help you with the sting operation."

Panic blooms within me as my heart sinks. "What? Oh no! Are you serious? Why not?"

At the moment, I'm parked in the large, wide circular courtyard in front of Lucretia Lux's beachfront mega mansion. I just arrived ten minutes ago and was about to call Officer Cuetee to get his estimated time of arrival when my cell phone rang.

I answered quickly, worried I might wake Callie, who fell into a deep, contented sleep moments after she announced that she'd be able to rest without worry because Officer Cuetee would be helping me with the sting operation.

Unfortunately, that's not the case.

"A bank in the Double H neighborhood was robbed an hour ago," says Officer Cuetee. "Most of the force was called to the scene. We're still here and I think we might be for a while."

"How long is a while, do you think?" I ask, hoping against hope even though I feel disappointment looming.

"I'm not sure," says Officer Cuetee.

"And you're sure you won't be able to help me with the sting?" I bite my lower lip, hoping he's not about to say what I'm sure he's going to say.

"I'm sorry," he says. "I know I won't. And ..."

"And?"

"And since I won't be able to help you then we'll have to put the sting off for now and do it another day," Officer Cuetee tells me.

Disappointed, I sigh. "I had a feeling you were going to say that."

"Listen, I know it's not what you wanted to hear," says Officer Cuetee. "But, I don't want you setting the trap for Esteban alone. If he's the killer—"

"I know he is," I say, staring at the steering wheel.

"Then he's dangerous," says Officer Cuetee. "I don't want him to hurt you."

"I don't want him to hurt me, either," I say.

"So ... we agree that we'll set the trap another day?"

Grudgingly, I say, "Okay, fine. I don't like it, but we can set the trap another day. But we have to do it soon. I have to call Esteban and tell him that I can't show up. He'll probably be suspicious and I'll have to convince him that my absence couldn't be avoided."

Chuckling, Officer Cuetee says, "Tell him that cat you know ran off and you need to find her."

Glancing at Callie, still curled up sleeping in the passenger seat, I say, "Well, she came back, so ..."

"Any idea where she was?"

"She didn't say," I tell him, biting my lip. "But I get the feeling—"

"She didn't say?"

Oops, I think. So much for my mental notes. I really need to organize them. Clearing my throat, I say, "Hey, look, I know you need to get back to keeping the streets of St. Mateo safe, and I need to call Esteban, so we'll talk later, okay? See ya!"

Disconnecting the call, I drop my phone into the cup holder

between the bucket seats and lean back against the headrest, closing my eyes.

To say I'm disappointed would be an understatement. I was sure Officer Cuetee and I would be able to trick Esteban into confessing to murder in exchange for Annie Stone's diary, which I don't have, but Esteban wouldn't know that, so …

So, now I have to call Esteban and give him some excuse as to why I can't show up today. Not sure what I'm going to tell him, but I have a sinking suspicion that he's going to be skeptical. Hopefully, I can put any doubts he may have to rest. If he refuses to meet with me again, then—

Several sharp, hard raps on my window cause me to jump.

I whip my head toward the sound.

A gasp escapes my lips.

The person standing outside my JEEP, knocking on the window, is Esteban.

But he wasn't knocking with his knuckles.

He was knocking with a large, black gun that he's pointing at me.

Instantly, my mouth goes dry and my heart slams. I can't think. What am I going to do? I want to stomp my foot down on the gas pedal and floor it. But I can't. After I arrived at Lucretia Lux's mansion, I cut the ignition to call Officer Cuetee. I don't know if I could—

"Get out of the car!" demands Esteban.

"What?" I ask, pretending not to hear him, even though the glass between us does nothing to suppress his harsh command. I'm stalling. Trying to buy myself time so I can start the JEEP and—

"I said get out of the car!"

The door opens. Balmy, ocean-scented air rushes into the JEEP as Esteban clamps a hand around my arm and yanks me from the car.

"Stop it!" I cry out, trying in vain to pull away from his vise-like grip. "Leave me alone! Get your hands off me!"

"Shut up!" Esteban growls as he drags me away from the car.

"Get away from me!" I yell, trying to fight him off. "Leave me—"

Esteban yanks me closer and presses the gun against my head. "Shut up or I will blow your head off!"

Scared silent, I comply with his demand, trying not to cry as he forces me toward the tall doors that open into the mansion. My heart lurches. I can't let him take me inside. If he does, I might never come out. But the gun is still pressed against my head, right above my ear. I can't scream or cry for help. I don't want to get shot. But I can't let him kill me. I have to think of something. And yet, all I can think is that I have to go through with the sting operation. I have to set the trap. And yes, I know I promised Officer Cuetee I wouldn't try to pull off the sting alone, but that was before Esteban dragged me from the car. Now, setting the trap might be the only way to save my life.

Seconds later, Esteban pushes me away to open the door.

I think of running, but he grabs me again and shoves me into the foyer.

"And don't bother screaming," he says, slamming the door closed. "Ms. Lux took a helicopter this morning to St. Felipe for some charity function and she's staying overnight."

My heart sinks.

"Now, where's Annie's diary," Esteban says, pulling me into the living room and over to one of the long, large, oversized couches.

"What?"

"Don't play stupid," he says, pushing me onto the couch. "Where is Annie's diary? You said you had it. Give it to me. Now."

"Right. Yes. Well ..." I clear my throat. "It's in my crossbody."

"I don't care where it is," he says, taking a few steps backward as he trains the gun on me. "Just hand it over."

"Well, I will have to remove it from my crossbody," I say, glancing down at my purse. "I don't want you to think I'm pulling out a weapon and—"

"Just give it to me!"

With shaking hands, I reach into my crossbody purse and feel around for my phone. Opening the purse so that I can see inside, I unlock the phone and activate my recording app.

"Where is the diary?" demands Esteban.

Sighing, I say, "Um … this is so super embarrassing, but … "

"But?"

"It's not in this purse," I tell him.

"Not in that purse?"

"It's in my other purse," I say. "See, I changed purses last night, and—"

"I don't care," says Esteban. "I just want the diary."

"Then you'll have to let me go home and get my other purse," I say.

Esteban shakes his head. "You've got to be kidding me."

"Well, you know," I say. "Now that I'm thinking about the diary … I'm not sure you need it."

"What do you mean?"

Clearing my throat, I say, "Well … if the cops find the diary, they might not suspect you."

"I thought you said that Annie identifies me as her stalker in the diary," says Esteban. "If the cops read her diary, they'll suspect that I killed her."

"Do you have an alibi for the murder?" I ask.

Shaking his head, Esteban says, "No, I don't."

"Well, could you come up with one?" I ask. "Because an alibi is really all you need to convince the police that you're innocent. What happened that night? You might have an alibi that you didn't know about."

Frowning, Esteban says, "I followed Annie to the dog park. I wanted to talk to her because she'd been avoiding me."

"You wanted to tell her you loved her?"

"And that I would do anything for her," says Esteban. "I wanted her to know that we belonged together. We were soulmates. I needed to convince her."

"What did Annie say when you told her that?"

Esteban scoffs. "She said what she always did. Said she would never be interested in dating me. She could never love me and never would. But I knew that wasn't true!"

"And then what happened?" I ask, hoping to keep him talking.

"She started saying crazy things," says Esteban, his expression hardening.

"What kind of crazy things?" I ask.

"She said I was a horrible person," he says, his eyes slightly unfocused. "She said I was unhinged. Psychotic. And then she said …"

"She said … what?" I prompt, focusing on the gun, which is only a tad bit lower. And despite the fact that Esteban looks as though he's reliving awful memories, I have no doubt that he'd snap out of his fog and shoot me in the back if I made a run for it. So, I stay put. For now.

"She said she hated me," he says, his voice vacant and hollow. "And then … "

Again, I prompt, "And then …?"

"I didn't mean to hurt her," says Esteban, his eyes shining with what appear to be tears. "I didn't want to hurt her. I loved her. But … the knife was in my hand and then … I was just trying to make her stop saying those awful things …"

"And you stabbed her so she would stop telling you that she hated you," I say.

"I didn't want to kill her," says Esteban. "But … "

"What about Novak Penegar?" I ask. "Did you want to kill him?"

Esteban's face morphs from grief to anger. "He deserved to die …"

"Why?" I ask, as Esteban paces back and forth.

"Because he kidnapped James Mortimer," says Esteban.

"Annie and Novak plotted James Mortimer's kidnapping together," I tell him.

Esteban stops pacing and glares at me. "That's not true."

"But it is true," I say. "I spoke to Novak and he told me—"

"Novak lied," thunders Esteban. "He forced Annie to help him."

I shake my head. "No, it was Annie's idea—"

"That's not true," insists Esteban. "Novak was a lying dognapper. And a blackmailer."

"A blackmailer?"

"Novak was there when I accidentally hurt Annie," says Esteban, resuming his pacing. "He had stolen the dog from Annie and was loitering in the dog park—"

"Actually, Novak was returning to get money from Annie for dog food when he saw you—"

"Believe that dognapper's lies, if you want," interrupts Esteban. "I don't care. But, he wanted money from me. If I didn't give it to him, he promised to tell the police that he saw me accidentally hurt Annie."

"Did you give him the blackmail money?"

"I told him I would," says Esteban. "But I never planned to pay him."

"You planned to kill him," I say.

"Because he … he … he … "

"He … what?"

Esteban's eyes flutter as he sniffs and clears his throat.

Frowning, I stare at the driver.

"He … he …" Esteban's eyes shut, his head whips back and he lets forth a volcanic sneeze that propels his body into a strange whirl.

"Oh my goodness!" I jump up, recognizing and remembering what's happening. Esteban is allergic to cats! The last time he dissolved into a sneezing fit was when Callie and I came to the mansion to question him before I knew him to be the ruthless, heartless killer of Annie Stone and Novak Penegar.

"Ah-CHOO!" sneezes Esteban, stumbling back, overtaken by the velocity of his sneeze.

At once it occurs to me that if Esteban is sneezing, there must be a cat nearby ...

Could it be Callie? Surreptitiously, I glance around the living room, searching for the feisty feline. She was still sleeping in the car when Esteban forced me out of the JEEP, and I'd assumed she was still there, but—

"Ah-CHOO!" Esteban flails around. "Cats ... there are ... ah-choo!"

"Are you okay?" I ask, keeping an eye on the gun, which Esteban still grips, but which he flings around as his body twists and bends from the propulsion of his sneezes.

"I ... I ... ah-CHOO!"

"Do you need your allergy medicine?" I ask, trying to inch backward, glancing toward the foyer, wondering if I should make a run for it. Wondering if—

"MEOWWWWWWWWWWWWWWWWWWW!!!!"

The feral feline cry sends a shudder through me.

"HELPPPPPPPPPPPPPPPPPPPPPPPPPPPP!!!!"

Esteban's panicked scream makes me shiver. I turn toward him and gasp ...

Callie launches toward Esteban, sinking her claws into his forehead as her feet pummel his chin and throat. Shouting his terror, Esteban drops to his knees, releasing the firearm, which tumbles across the hardwood floor.

Seconds later, I gasp again, this time in shock as an orange cat joins Callie in the assault, lunging at Esteban's back. Hanging onto the driver's shirt, the orange cat sinks its teeth into Esteban's neck.

"Help … get them off me!" shouts Esteban between sneezes.

Callie and the orange cat continue their attack and are joined by three more cats—a black and white cat, a sleek gray cat, and a white cat with brown patches. For the next few minutes, I watch in awe as Callie and the other four cats, growling and meowing, beat Esteban into a whimpering, sneezing submission.

"Call the cops, girl!" commands Callie as she releases her hold on Esteban, jumps off him, and trots toward me. "And get the gun!

"Right, right …" I scramble over to the gun, pick it up, and then race over to the couch where I grab my phone from my purse. As Callie directs the cats to back away from Esteban—after all, he's not in a position to do anything other than sneeze—I call the police.

Epilogue

"So, once again, the cat that you know that's not really your cat saved the day, huh?" says Officer Cuetee, giving me a cute, sly smile.

"She absolutely did!" I say, glancing into the backseat of Officer Cuetee's squad car, where both Dutiful, the Belgian Malinois, and Callie, are sleeping.

Three days have passed since Callie and her fierce feline friends attacked Esteban, bringing the murdering stalker to his knees. After I called the cops, they showed up and after I gave my statement, they took Esteban to the police station for questioning.

"Callie showed up with four other cats," I say. "They pounced on Esteban and with his cat allergies, there was no way for him to fight back."

"Well, I'm glad you're okay," he says, turning off the side road and onto the coastal highway that rings the island. "But, I am upset that I wasn't there to protect you from Esteban."

"I know," I say, giving him an encouraging smile. "But, there was no way to know that Esteban would pull me out of the car. He came from nowhere. I'm thinking he was lurking outside. Watching me. After all, he is a stalker."

"And a killer," says Officer Cuetee. "The murder weapon—the Swiss Army knife—used to kill Annie Stone and Novak Penegar was found in Esteban's room at the mansion. And, there's also exterior and interior surveillance which shows Esteban entering the mansion the night Annie was killed."

"You're kidding," I say.

"The video that gave Lucretia Lux an alibi is the same video that proves Esteban is a killer," says Officer Cuetee. "In the video, Annie Stone leaves the house with James Mortimer an hour or so before midnight. Then ten minutes later, Esteban leaves the mansion, presumably to follow Annie. An hour or so after midnight, Esteban returns to the mansion. When he exits the car, he's holding an object. Video enhancements show it to be the Swiss Army knife. But then Esteban leaves the house again and returns about twenty minutes later."

"Why?" I ask. "Where did he go?"

"When Francois questioned Esteban yesterday, he caved." Officer Cuetee uses his indicator to switch lanes. "Esteban admitted that he was going to try to frame Chef Bonnie for Annie's murder. When he left the house a second time, it was because he'd taken one of Chef Bonnie's knives and took it back to the scene of the crime."

"So that's how Chef Bonnie's knife was discovered in the park," I say, chilled by Esteban's diabolical treachery.

Nodding, Officer Cuetee says, "Esteban knew Annie and Chef Bonnie had beef."

"Annie was blackmailing Chef Bonnie," I say, "which gave Chef Bonnie a motive to kill Annie."

"Right," says Officer Cuetee. "And Esteban knew Chef Bonnie's prints were likely to be on her own knife. He almost got away with murder and might have if not for you."

"Me?"

Smiling, Officer Cuetee says, "Francois confronted him with that recording from your app."

Shaking my head, I say, "Can't believe I had the presence of mind to start the recording."

"Well, there's enough evidence for the prosecutor to present an airtight case against Esteban," says Officer Cuetee. "Anyway, now … on to today's adventure."

"Thanks for helping me with this," I say, taking another glance back at Callie. The Calico is still napping peacefully, unaware that we might be about to find out who her real owner is …

Yesterday, over tea during lunch, I told Officer Cuetee about Walter Wagner, the dead man whose car was used by an unknown person to drive to the animal shelter and abandon Callie. Officer Cuetee promised to look into Walter Wagner and discovered that the title of his car was transferred to his son, Walter Wagner Jr.

Further investigation of Walter Jr. revealed his employment at a Hullabaloo Coffee Shop on the southern tip of St. Mateo, which is where Officer Cuetee and I are heading on an overcast Saturday afternoon.

Twenty minutes later, we arrive. Officer Cuetee stays in the car while I hurry inside. The coffee shop bustles with activity. Maneuvering between tourists and locals, I head toward a barista cleaning a small wooden bistro table in the corner.

"Excuse me …" I approach the barista. "Can you tell me if Walter is working today?"

"I think he's on a break," says the barista. "I'll send him over."

Moments later, when a slight, pimple-faced guy slinks toward me, I introduce myself and state my business.

Shoulders slumped, Walter Jr. says, "I know the cat you're talking about."

My heart starts to pound. "Is Callie your cat?"

Walter Jr. shakes his head. "I'm sorry about what I did but I didn't know what to do. That Calico was abandoned in the men's room."

"Abandoned in the men's room?" I asked, confused and shocked.

"I found her one night after we'd closed the shop," says Walter. "Walked into the men's room to clean up. Heard meowing from one of the stalls. Opened the stall door and there was the Calico in a cat carrier. I took the cat to the shelter when I left work, but it was after midnight. The shelter was closed, so I just left the cat there."

Worried and intrigued, I ask, "And you have no idea who left the cat in the men's room?"

Walter Jr. says, "None whatsoever. But the shop is always so busy. And people bring animals in here all the time, so it wouldn't have been out of the norm to see someone with a cat."

After thanking Walter Jr., and grabbing two chai lattes for myself and Officer Cuetee, I walk out of the shop with more questions than answers.

I was so certain that Walter Jr. could help me solve the mystery of Callie's real owner, but I'm more perplexed than ever. All I know is that someone left Callie in the coffee shop restroom. Well, actually, that's not all I know. I also know that Callie was in a cat carrier. That leads me to believe that she was left behind by someone who cared enough to buy her a carrier. And who would do that if not the person who owned her?

Then again, the person who left her might not have been the owner. Maybe the owner asked the person who left Callie to watch her. And then, what if the owner never came back for Callie? So the person watching her decided to leave her behind in a bathroom.

Then again, suppose Callie was catnapped. And maybe the catnapper got nervous and abandoned her in the men's bathroom.

Or, maybe … maybe I need to discuss this with Officer Cuetee. Once I report to him what Walter Jr. told me, I am sure he'll have some theories and we can—

As I approach Officer Cuetee's car, I slow my stride, confusion rocking me, making my heart pound.

Staring at the vehicle, I peer into the windows as I circle the car, trying to make sense of what I'm seeing.

Or, rather, trying to figure out what I'm not seeing ...

Officer Cuetee, Callie, and Dutiful.

The car is empty.

The dreamboat, the sassy cat, and the faithful dog are gone ...

Ready for another exciting "tail" from Sophie and Callie?

Check out their next mystery in A Dark and Devious Tail.

A controversial clinic. A swarm of bees. A sticky situation with more twists and turns than a ball of yarn.

A Dark and Devious Tail is the delightful fourth book in the high-spirited Sassy Sarcastic Cat Cozy Mysteries.

Immerse yourself in a world of enigmatic secrets, a talking cat, and twists as intriguing as a curling feline tail.

Join Sophie and Callie in untangling a web of clues, solving puzzling crimes, and chasing leads darker than the night. This is your invitation to dive into a gripping cozy mystery that will keep you hooked from start to finish. Don't miss your chance – grab your copy now and prepare for a reading experience that's as spellbinding as it is purr-fect!

Buy A Dark and Devious Tail to pounce on the truth today!

https://geni.us/darkanddevioustail

Hey, y'all, hey!!!

Subscribe to my newsletter and you'll get inspiring rescue stories, hilarious cat memes, and thrilling serialized fiction. Plus, you can find out first about new books featuring my fabulous life as a feisty, fierce feline, and much more!

Sign me up!

Sassy Callie

https://subscribepage.io/SassyCallie

Also by Rachel Woods

SASSY SARCASTIC CAT COZY MYSTERIES

Sophie Carter, a struggling reporter for the *Palmchat Gazette*, teams up with a sassy talking Calico cat to solve crimes as she strives to become an influential investigative reporter

A SLY AND SINISTER TAIL

A COLD AND CUNNING TAIL

A FOUL AND FEARSOME TAIL

A DARK AND DEVIOUS TAIL

REPORTER ROLAND BEAN COZY MYSTERIES

Roland "Beanie" Bean, husband and loving father, finds himself the unwitting participant in solving crimes as he seeks to make a name for himself as a reporter for the *Palmchat Gazette*.

HAPPY BIRTHDAY MURDER

EASTER EGG HUNT MURDER

MERRY CHRISTMAS MURDER

TRICK OR TREAT MURDER

GOBBLE GOBBLE MURDER

HAPPY 4TH OF JULY MURDER

SUMMER VACATION MURDER

HAPPY NEW YEAR MURDER

PALMCHAT ISLANDS MYSTERIES

Married journalists, Vivian and Leo, manage the island newspaper while solving crimes as they chase leads for their next story.

UNTIL DEATH DO US PART

NO ONE WILL FIND YOU

YOU WILL DIE FOR THIS

DON'T MAKE ME HURT YOU

THE PALMCHAT ISLANDS MYSTERIES BOX SET: BOOKS 1 - 4

RUTHLESS REVENGE ROMANCE SERIES

Gripping romantic suspense series with steamy romance, unpredictable plot twists and devastating consequences of deceit.

HER DEADLY MISTAKE

HER DEADLY DECEPTION

HER DEADLY THREAT

HER DEADLY BETRAYAL

MURDER IN PARADISE SERIES

A series of stand-alone women sleuth mysteries with murder, mayhem and a dash of romance, set against the backdrop of turquoise waters and swaying palm trees of the fictional Palmchat Islands.

THE UNWORTHY WIFE

THE SILENT ENEMY

THE PERFECT LIAR

About the Author

Rachel Woods studied journalism and graduated from the University of Houston where she published articles in the Daily Cougar. She is a legal assistant by day and a freelance writer and blogger with a penchant for melodrama by night. Many of her stories take place on the islands, which she has visited around the world. Rachel resides in Houston, Texas with her three sock monkeys.

For more information:
www.therachelwoods.com
rachel@therachelwoods.com

facebook.com/therachelwoodsauthor
instagram.com/therachelwoodsauthor
bookbub.com/authors/rachel-woods
amazon.com/author/therachelwoods

About the Publisher

BONZAIMOON BOOKS

BonzaiMoon Books is a family-run, artisanal publishing company created in the summer of 2014. We publish works of fiction in various genres. Our passion and focus is working with authors who write the books you want to read, and giving those authors the opportunity to have more direct input in the publishing of their work.

For more information:
www.bonzaimoonbooks.com
info@bonzaimoonbooks.com

facebook.com/BonzaiMoonBooks
x.com/bonzaimoon

www.ingramcontent.com/pod-product-compliance
Lightning Source LLC
Chambersburg PA
CBHW071149180726
48291CB00007B/2394